DESTINY

DESTINY

THE GIRL IN THE BOX
BOOK NINE

Robert J. Crane

DESTINY
THE GIRL IN THE BOX
BOOK NINE

Copyright © 2014 Reikonos Press
All Rights Reserved.

1st Edition

AUTHOR'S NOTE

This book is a work of fiction. Names, characters, places and incidents are products of the author's imagination or are used fictitiously. Any resemblance to actual events or locales or persons, living or dead, is entirely coincidental.

The scanning, uploading and distribution of this book via the internet or any other means without the permission of the publisher is illegal and punishable by law. Please purchase only authorized electronic editions, and do not participate in or encourage electronic piracy of copyrighted materials. Your support of the author's rights is appreciated.

No part of this publication may be reproduced in whole or in part without the written permission of the publisher. For information regarding permission, please email cyrusdavidon@gmail.com

This book is dedicated to Nicholas J. Ambrose, who was my editor, cover artist and formatter before he was my friend, and who helped me build the confidence that publishing was easy until I was in too deep to know better. Without him, my career would not be nearly so far along as it is.

Acknowledgments

Karri Klawiter once again worked magic with a cover, and with so little to work on she might as well be a meta herself. An art-creating meta. Hmm, I think I just had a book idea...

Sarah Barbour once more worked diligently to minimize the ass I make of myself with my words. It's a hard job, but she really does well with it.

Jo Evans, Erin Kane and Jessica Kelishes gave the manuscript an added level of polish and helped me iron out those last creeping errors.

Thanks also to my wife and kids, who make it all possible and worthwhile.

Lastly, thanks to my parents, who were present for the last week of the writing this book and helped immensely. We had a baby born on Monday and I finished writing the book with a marathon session on Saturday. That wouldn't have happened without their help.

291-9849

Chapter 1

CHARLIE

Charlie screamed as she got cut; a long, searing slice up her belly that felt like someone squirted lighter fluid into it, lit a match and tossed it in. The slash shredded her blouse and she staggered back from her attacker, gasping.

He was big. The kind of big that would stand out on any street. Any street but this one, maybe.

Charlie turned and ran without a thought. When it came to fight or flight, her choice was always easy. The warm, dry desert air of the Las Vegas night hit her cheeks. Searing pain ran through her abdomen, and she could feel the blood running down to her jeans.

She was on the Strip, the heavy heat of day gone hours ago, disappearing after nightfall. With every step she ran, she felt the pain of the open wound. The nearby neon display of the Mirage Casino flashed at her as her feet pounded against the concrete.

Charlie tossed a look back over her shoulder. She hadn't seen the guy coming. She'd been staggering under one of the footbridges near Caesar's Palace, embracing the swirling feel of having a good drunk on. Her head was light from the booze some guy had bought her to get her pants off and from the feeling of his soul swimming around inside her after she'd let him think he'd get his way.

Just another mark. Just another night.

Charlie sprinted up the strip. It was the wee hours of the morning, five or so, and day was about to break over the horizon. All that sweet euphoria from the grifted alcohol and the stolen soul had evaporated when that big guy had come at her. She hadn't even noticed him until it was too late. Hadn't even seen the knife.

All she knew was that it hurt.

The Mirage had flown past on her left and now she was crossing in front of Treasure Island. The taste of that heavy martini was still lingering on her tongue. She could smell a Starbucks ahead, could feel the burn on her stomach. She'd gotten attacked back at the edge of the Caesar's Palace property. She'd run far, and fast. Meta speed. Hadn't even cared if anyone had seen her.

She slowed, looking over her shoulder. There was nothing; just the normal street wanderers, drunks and vagrants asking for weed money, beer money, or gambling money. And few enough of them at this hour. Even the bachelor parties had ended by this point, surely.

Charlie tried to catch her breath. It was coming in hard gasps, the sound blotting out everything going on around her. She ran a hand over her injury. She kept walking fast and dodged around the next footbridge before she stopped.

Charlie leaned back against the grey, two-story concrete footbridge. Escalators ran up and down, ferrying passengers to the top so they could cross the road in peace and continue spending their gambling and drinking dollars without a trip to the emergency room from getting run over by one of Vegas's crazed taxi drivers. Charlie liked the footbridges. They were a great place to brush past people, touching them as she went.

Charlie looked down. The blood had soaked her front, had run all the way down and darkened the denim of her jeans. Her blouse had already been red; now it bore a darker stain starting just underneath her right breast. She ran a finger through the hole where it had been shredded open. Pain greeted her.

This would heal, probably before the end of the day. Her breathing started to slow. It wasn't about the wound. This was minor. It was an inconvenience.

It was really about the fact that someone had dared to come at her. Who would do that?

Vegas was *her* town. Had been—on and off—for years. Whenever the heat got too high anywhere else, this was the place Charlie knew she could go. She'd had to dye her hair once or twice, change her look, but mostly Vegas was her safe ground.

Someone attacking her here? And worse, some human with a knife?

Charlie felt her breath turn hot. She felt a seething anger come, along with her searing pain.

Nobody did this to her. Not to her.

She slapped a bloody palm against the grey footbridge wall as she leaned against it.

The fury was growing inside her. She'd jumped at something minor. Jackrabbited when she should have grabbed the knife out of that big bastard's hand and then showed him what happened to people who messed with her. It could have been slow, dragging. She could have teased his soul out of him for hours that would feel like an eternity.

Charlie called it foreplay. Whatever other succubi called it (she'd never really talked it over with her sister—that stick in the mud—or her pathetic daughter), it was damned fun.

When she caught up with the big guy, she was going to have a hell of a lot of foreplay.

She could drag him back to her hotel room. It wasn't that far, just a mile or so off the Strip. She liked the motels off the strip. Less security. Fewer cameras.

Less for the police to work with when a body turned up in a dumpster.

She slapped her palm against the footbridge again. This bastard was gonna pay when she caught him. Slow and fun, that's how she'd make it.

Charlie tensed her abdomen, tested the pain. It was manageable. She gritted her teeth and breathed out again. Yeah. She could do this.

She started to push off the wall, ready to turn the corner and run back down the Strip toward Caesar's when a hand caught her around the throat. It wore a leather glove that she could feel against the skin of her neck, and slammed her into the concrete wall of the footbridge with enough force to snap her head back.

"This is her, right?" came a voice from the shadowed face above her. Charlie's head was swimming, and not just from the booze and soul now. A trickle of blood ran down the back of her head, tickling her neck.

"Yeah." The answering voice was even deeper than the first. Charlie's eyes were so blurry she couldn't see the man who had her, let alone the one behind him that answered. "Charlene Nealon."

"Who are you?" Charlie's question dribbled out. She was dimly aware that something was wrong, really wrong.

"You fractured her skull," the shadow in back said.

"I know," the guy in front replied. "It was fun. Better than that little scratch you gave her."

Charlie raised a hand, tried to land it on the guy's wrist. She felt leather, warm, like a biker jacket. Her fingers kneaded the material, trying to rip through it. The pressure increased around her throat.

"Think I'll just choke her out," the guy in front said. He was so shadowed she couldn't see anything other than he was clean-shaven. Charlie's fingers probed near his hand, trying to find the gap between his glove and jacket. *If I can just ...*

"I wouldn't give her the chance if I were you," the guy in back said. He sounded ... gruffer, somehow. Through blurred eyes she could see red hair framing his face.

"Right." The man in shadow slammed her head into the concrete again and Charlie's hand dropped. Her eyes were blurrier now. Something warm and wet was sliding down the back of her neck now. Her mouth twitched.

"Again," Red said. This time Charlie barely felt it as her head hit the footbridge again. The sound it made was loud, though, and she felt something wet hit her cheek. "You're taking it awfully easy on her," Red said from behind Shadow. "Three hits and you've yet to splatter her brains all over the place."

"I like to take it slow," Shadow said. "Really make them suffer."

"Sounds familiar," Red said, and he didn't sound impressed. "Just get it over with already. We've got business in Minneapolis."

"Fine," Shadow said, and his irritation was not lost even on Charlie. Her eyes could barely make out his silhouette anymore. She couldn't breathe, but she couldn't fight against him, either. Her body was not in her control, not anymore. "Say goodnight, Charlie."

She wanted to laugh. It was like that old George Burns joke. She felt the corner of her mouth creep up in a smile.

Her head swayed forward one last time then was thrown back into the concrete, and everything went dark.

Chapter 2

SIENNA

I stared out my office window across the campus of the Metahuman Policing and Threat Response Task Force. It was an awkward mouthful to say all that, so like everyone else around here I'd just taken to calling it "the Agency." The moon was rising outside my window, shedding a dull glow over the dormitory building in the distance. Beyond that, floodlights glowed around the construction site that had been our future science building. I could see figures moving around next to the concrete walls like ants swarming out of an anthill.

I wished I was one of them. Small enough to escape notice, small enough to be able to leave my office and have no one realize I was even gone. I could just follow the next ant in line in front of me and not even worry about where I was going. It would be freedom. I could disappear into the tall trees of the forest beyond, never to be seen again. Not that the other ants would notice me anyway.

My head was heavy on the leather chair back. My eyes shut themselves part way of their own accord, and the scent of leather from my furniture was in the air. This was my office. My responsibilities were as present as the smell of leather.

And silence reigned all around me.

"So ..." the voice of my brother, Reed Treston, filled the air. "Is anyone gonna say anything?"

I swiveled slowly around, leaving the window and its picturesque view behind me. The office was cramped by comparison. Reed was standing by the door, but he was hardly alone. Ariadne Fraser sat in the chair in front of me, her pale face and red hair in marked contrast to each other. My mother, Sierra Nealon, waited on the wall opposite Reed nearest the door, her arms folded and her head back against the wall in much the same way I suspected my head had been against the chair only a moment earlier.

Agent Li of the FBI, my liaison with the US government, was in the chair next to Ariadne. He was watching me through half-lidded eyes, and I couldn't tell whether he was skeptical or suspicious. Directly behind him was Scott Byerly—blond-haired, tall, muscular. I may have let my eyes linger on him just a second longer than necessary before moving on.

Finally, on the couch next to my mother sat a couple. One of them looked young, like a little blond cheerleader pulled off the local JV team. She was thin, pretty and perky. Kat Forrest. The guy next to her could have been her grandfather, but he wasn't. He was likely much older than any grandfather she might have had.

"Janus," Ariadne said, glancing back at him.

"Ariadne Fraser," Janus said with a nod to her. "It is a pleasure to finally make your acquaintance after many years of hearing about your skill and capability." Janus's words were characterized by a thick European accent that I'd never been able to place.

"I'm touched - and obviously unsurprised - that Omega was spying on me," Ariadne said with a low voice, filled with loathing. "Can you tell us if Sienna can use her powers the way Sovereign does?"

"Ah," Janus said, and his lips pursed in a pained way. "That is an excellent question. I believe she can. Hades was very capable of using the powers of the meta souls he absorbed, though how he did it is a bit of mystery."

"Why is it so mysterious?" Scott asked. Every eye in the place was on Janus.

Janus looked around, still worn and tired-looking, with dark bags under his eyes. “Because we—the powerful, that is to say—the gods and then, later, Omega—did everything we could to make certain such knowledge was lost. Incubi and succubi were wiped out in large numbers following the death of Hades. They found themselves unwelcome in communities of metas.” He glanced at me. “Perhaps you have felt some of this stigma yourself?”

My mother grunted. “Succubi are outcasts? You don’t say.”

“It was all very deliberate,” Janus said, sparing only a look at her. “The old gods were certain that they never killed all the children of Hades. There were so many, after all. But very few of them ever demonstrated the ability to use the powers of other metas, so it was determined that we would kill when necessary and merely shun the rest. It is a method that has worked for several thousand years with only one unfortunate exception in that time.” He sighed deeply, his shoulders slumping. “It would appear that exception, however, is perhaps the most damning evidence that they should have persisted in wiping out the rest, as he seems hell-bent on repaying the favor on the rest of metakind with an abundance of gusto.”

“I can’t imagine why he’d be upset,” Reed said, arms folded over his leather jacket, ponytail tucked back behind him. “You bastards at Omega and your predecessors were only responsible for the suppression and partial extermination of his people.”

“To be fair, I had nothing to do with it,” Janus said, almost indifferent. “Although I think we can see now that there may have been some merit to the concern that an incubus or succubus who could freely combine the powers of the metas they absorb would be extraordinarily dangerous.”

“Because you made him dangerous,” Reed said with disgust. “You people have always been about protecting your own power. You couldn’t have an army of incubi and succubi out there absorbing other metas because if you did, you might lose control.

It might eat into your profit margin, might start breaking that tight leash you had around our kind. This is all about power, about depriving people of it for your own purposes—"

"Reed," my mother said, more gently than I would have given her credit for. "He's right. Think of what that power could do in the wrong hands. Imagine Charlie with the power of … I don't know, that flame-guy Sienna killed. Or the rock-head you used to have around here—"

"Who Sienna also killed," Li muttered under his breath. Everyone heard him, but no one said anything.

"So," Ariadne said, and I felt every eye in the place turn to her. It was almost like I could see their thoughts, as one, ratcheting around like gears in a clock, the hands clicking around to point at me. "Can you?"

I stared at her, feeling completely dull of wit. Could I? It was a valid question. "I don't know. Maybe."

I watched Reed turn to my mother. "What about you? Can you use another meta's power?"

My mother took a breath, and her eyes got wide as I saw her think about it. "I can't recall a time when I've even felt a hint of it. Of course, I've only absorbed a couple metas, and only in dire straits. I'm honestly not even sure what type one of them is; the other is a Selene-type, which is pretty rare, as I understand it."

"What does a … Selene-type do?" Ariadne asked with a frown.

My mother gave a light shrug. "Named for the Greek goddess of the moon. Near as I could tell, basically … she could glow in the dark." Scott snickered. "She was still wicked strong, but I'm guessing her power was of a lot more use before the invention of the incandescent bulb. Could have been helpful when an army was marching off to war in the darkness. Now?" Her eyes moved around the room. "Not so much."

"Assuming you could tap into those powers," Ariadne said, thin fingers on her chin in contemplation, "you'd be able to fill the air with a faint glow and … possibly do something else." She sighed. "That's not exactly going to win the war against the seemingly invulnerable Sovereign."

"The good news is," Scott said, and I could feel the room turning back to me again, "we've got another succubus, and this one has absorbed a Djinn-type, a Fae-type, a Quetzalcoatl, an Odin-type and … whatever the hell Wolfe was."

"Cerberus is the technical name, I believe," my mother said. "I think there were only ever the three of them, though."

"Their father was one as well, but he is dead," Janus said with a light nod of acknowledgment toward my mother. "Hades had the three brothers castrated with a sword set aflame by Hephaestus before they entered his service because he did not wish to suffer a scenario in which another of their kind might be born from actions taken in the course of their … activities."

Reed cleared his throat. "Which is the most polite way I've ever heard it put that Wolfe is probably history's most prolific serial killer and rapist. Though, for my money, if Hades had had the meat cut off with the potatoes it might have spared the world an awful lot of misery." He glanced at me.

I didn't meet his gaze. I stared at the blank, white desk calendar that sat in front of me.

"Sienna?" Ariadne spoke. I did not look up. "Are you sure you can't …?"

"I don't know," I said again, and I barely recognized my own voice. "Maybe. I think Wolfe might have used his powers through me, once." I glanced at Kat, then Scott. "During the fight with Gavrikov and Henderschott on top of the IDS Tower. I think he … took me over and used his power to heal me. But I've never …" I looked to Ariadne, "… never been able to do it myself."

There was another pause. A silence that told me that everyone else was hesitant to push further. I kept my eyes down.

Scott spoke. "Can I just say it?" He hesitated. "That the reason

Sovereign was after Sienna—"

"I think we're all up to speed on that now," my mother interrupted.

"Maybe," Scott said, "but—I mean, this is major. We've been running around this entire time wondering what motivates this guy, what weakness he might have since he hasn't shown anything so far—"

"We get it," my mother said again, her voice getting darker. I could see the clouds moving in across her forehead.

"Do you?" Scott said, turning to face her. "Do you really? Because I think it came as a little bit of a surprise to me, and it occurs to me you probably haven't had to deal with this particular kind of scrutiny from another meta ever before—"

"You think this is the first time an incubus has come at a succubus for this purpose?" My mother's voice carried more than just the seeds of umbrage. I recognized her tone as one that meant Scott was heading toward dangerous territory. More than a few times I'd heard her like this just before I had a metal door slammed in my face.

"Can we just say it?" Scott asked. "He—"

"Don't," my mother said, and her voice was as cold and unyielding as the door of the box had been in all the days of my youth.

"Someone should," Reed said, nearly whispering. "Someone should say it out loud, just because … this is … I mean, this is huge. Heinous, but huge. Sovereign has been waiting—"

"Stop," my mother hissed.

"—searching for centuries, or maybe even millennia—"

"SHUT UP!" My mother's voice rose to a shout. "STOP—"

"He's been looking for her," Reed said, "going through candidates one by one for however long—"

"STOP TALKING! JUST STOP—"

I brought my hand down on my desk and slammed it hard into

the wood. I didn't crack it, but it made a thunderous noise as I slapped my palm against the surface. I looked at the faces around me, my little crew.

Less than an hour earlier, I'd stared into the face of the man who'd been called the most dangerous metahuman in the world.

Had stared into his face and seen…something…I hadn't seen in a long while.

"I know why he's after me," I said, looking from Li, who was focused on his shoes, to Ariadne, who stared at me with dull eyes. "I know how he's treated me compared to others he's clashed with." I glanced at Kat, holding tight to Janus on the couch. They were both watching, listening. "I saw in his eyes what he wanted from me." I let my gaze drift to Reed, who wore something approaching a look of pity, then to my mother across the door frame. "I felt his intentions in the way he talked, the way he deferred to me."

Finally my eyes came around to Scott, who had one hand in his tousled, sandy-blond hair. He looked back at me with pity, too, but something else. Something that had been purer in its expression only a few hours earlier, when he kissed me. Something that had been missing from my life for … months. I licked my lips, and it felt like I could taste his kiss still lingering there, as though he had just done it a moment earlier.

And I thought of Sovereign, of how I'd touched him, stood only inches away while trying to drain the life from him. Foolishly, it turned out.

"I know you didn't intend for that to be meaningful," he'd said to me, *"but for me it kind of was."*

"I know what he wants from me," I said, and I looked at Scott. He looked back, and I could see the dread forming in his eyes. I tried to decide whether it came from what I was saying, or whether it was a reflection of what he saw from me. Either way, it didn't matter. Not really. "He wants me … to be his. His consort." I said it clinically. Emotionless.

"His … companion." I felt the bile in the back of my throat as the words rolled out of my mouth. "His … wife." The acrid taste in my mouth grew stronger at this thought, and one final pronouncement came ringing out, making me positively nauseous from top to bottom. "His lover."

Chapter 3

The night air was quiet and fresh. I took a deep breath and exhaled, taking it into my lungs. My knees rested on the ground, my jeans pushing against the hard dirt floor of the woods.

I was in the forest that ringed the campus, my eyes closed as I knelt on the ground. The taste of that last cup of coffee was still with me. I hated the stuff, but I'd needed it in order to avoid sleep. My body had threatened to crash after the meeting had broken up in the wake of my grim pronouncement, and I wasn't ready to sleep. Not yet.

I had things to do.

I took another breath and squinted my eyes closed. Crickets chirped around me in the warm summer air, and I let one of my hands touch the dirt, running my fingers over the forest floor. A dew-soaked blade of grass brushed my palm, and I felt the water run down to the tip of my index finger.

I looked deep inside, into a swirling darkness that was blacker than the night around me. I could withdraw into myself when necessary, into a little space that I'd set aside, and it was almost like retreating from the world. There was no smell, no taste but what I brought with me.

All that surrounded me was a circle of six metal monuments, each taller than me.

Faint howls echoed, voices raised in a cacophony that was muted by the walls of the metal boxes that imprisoned the souls I carried with me. I took a breath as I sat in the center of the circle and rose from the kneeling position I was in.

I turned and looked at each of the steel sarcophagi in turn. They were perfect recreations. Massive, dark-blue plates welded together at the corners, six feet tall, with a little window on the front of each. I gestured to the one behind me and it opened with a click, the lock sliding free. Hinges squealed as the door opened.

"I'm not sorry to get out of there," Zack said, stepping free of his prison. His blond hair was neat, and he was wearing a suit. Just like I remembered him.

"You saw everything?" I asked. I thought I could feel shame burning my cheeks.

"Yeah," he said, and his teeth gritted together in a grimace. "He's been after you this whole time so you'd be his child bride, huh?"

"So it would seem."

"Hmm." Zack took another step toward me, scratching his nose. Why did he do that? I wondered. It wasn't like he had an actual, physical nose that itched anymore. "You're gonna need help from the inmates."

I looked in a slow circle around the metal prisons I'd built to house my mental squatters. "You think they'll jump at the chance to give me a hand?"

"Not likely," Zack said with a shake of his head. "Not after you figured out how to toss us all in stir."

I stared at him. He really was just as handsome as he'd ever been outside of my head. "*You* don't seem that bitter about it."

"I … was in love with you," Zack said with a faint smile. "And I betrayed you when we first got started, if you recall, so my guilt might be weighing in your favor. It's not like I enjoy being in there." He gestured to the open cell behind him. "But I know how important it is for you to be able to think clearly, so I accept my punishment like … well, like the guilty party I am, I guess."

"It's not a punishment," I said quietly.

"It's fate, then," he said. "And I am resigned to my fate."

I gave the circle of steel boxes around me another look. "Let's see if anyone else feels the same." I gestured my hand in a slow circle and the locks for every one of the cages clicked open.

One of the doors opened immediately, with a thud, and I turned to see Bjorn's muscular body sweep out of the box, shirtless, chest bulging. "Ah, the air of freedom. How can it be so stale and dank in place that does not truly exist?"

The door next to his clanked open and a lithe, nude female form stepped out. "Haven't you realized yet? We are in hell, and the dankness is as close to brimstone as you'll get." Her blond hair was still pixie-short and grew in several other places I didn't need to see, like her armpits and … further south.

"God, Eve, put some clothes on, will you?" I flung a hand at her and a moment later she was clad in a t-shirt and jeans. Better than the nothing she apparently preferred.

"You seem to have come in contact with the enemy." Roberto Bastian's enclosure swung open with a squeak, and he gently closed it behind him once he was out. "And your plan didn't survive."

"No plan does," I said tersely as I looked at the former leader of M-Squad. "Or so I've heard."

"My sister is well, it would seem." Aleksandr Gavrikov spoke from behind me. I felt my jaw clench at the mere mention of his sister. It wasn't that I was even annoyed by her anymore; it was that he wouldn't EVER shut up about her.

"She's fine," I said, composing myself rather than just flinging him back into the box he'd stepped out of. I counted them off in my head, one by one. Five of them were out of their cages. One to go.

Of course it was *him*.

There was no light in the darkness, but I could still see each of their faces as though a lamp followed my gaze. I looked at each of them in turn then I swiveled to face the last box.

The lock was undone but the door was closed. I stared, willing it to open, and it did, noiselessly. I could see his shadow within, could almost see his eyes gleaming inside the box.

Watching me. Judging me. Sizing me up. The most heinous creature I'd ever met.

"Wolfe …" I said, "Aren't you going to come out and play?"

Chapter 4

"Maybe the Wolfe doesn't want to come out and play anymore, Little Doll." The voice was little more than a rasp, and lacked all the vigor and laughing cruelty that had always been present in his speech. The darkness enshrouded him, he was wrapped up in it, and even though I could feel him watching, I couldn't see him.

A little chill made its way over my body. "Wolfe doesn't want to come out and play?" I took a step closer to the box, but no more of him was revealed than had been before. "You just want to … sit in there and think about what you've done?" I took another step closer, heard my footstep click over the silence of the others, who were watching quietly. "Are you just going to sit in there and play with yourself?"

I heard a faint growl, but it ended within seconds. "The Wolfe grows tired of the Little Doll's plans. The Little Doll's prison."

I clenched my jaw again. He revolted me. Every moment of every day for the rest of my life, I would have been content to let him sit in the box in my head, out of my sight and as near to out of my mind as I could get him.

But it wasn't that easy.

"Sovereign," I said, saying the name almost as much to remind myself of why I had deigned to come in here and talk to these disembodied vagrants as to focus the conversation. "You know he's an incubus."

Wolfe's shadow didn't move. "Didn't know. Don't care."

The circle of the others that surrounded me was silent. "What about the rest of you?" I asked. "Do any of you care?"

"No," Eve Kappler replied, tugging at the bottom of the grey t-shirt I'd forced on her like she was trying to test the fabric for flaws. "I don't care if he makes you his whore for the rest of your days—"

I waved a hand and Eve was propelled backward, into the box from whence she'd come. I slammed the door on her and the lock fell back into place with only a thought from me. The sound of the metal clang echoed through the darkness. "Let me make this clear … I'm not going to be anyone's whore." I stared at each of them in turn with a burning glare. "Not his. And certainly not yours. I need help, but I don't need it bad enough to take shit from any you."

"I think you do," Bjorn said, and I turned to look at him. He'd towered over me in life, a mountain of a man. "You need us. And I want to hear you … beg for help." He grew a slow smile, and the air turned frosted around us as he let a long breath of white mist.

I clenched my fist and felt myself swell. Bjorn was an animal, a beast so low as to be worthy only of eating off the ground and rooting through his own feces for nourishment. I knew what he'd done in life, and in my view he was as pathetic as Wolfe.

"Let me tell you something about begging," I said as he began to shrink before me. It wasn't something he did voluntarily; but this was my mind, and I controlled it. I grew to twice his size and stared down at him. He was barely up to my waist at this point. I reached out and grabbed him around the neck with one hand, hauling him off his feet and into the air. I stared into his wide eyes. "If anyone's going to beg in here, it will be you—and it will be for mercy."

I squeezed him and his eyes bulged. I could feel his pain but I blanketed him with quiet. His soul screamed with agony, but no one could hear him save for me. I kept a lid on it. It swelled, like a pressure cooker reaching its limits, a faint shrieking, barely audible. Finally, I let it loose and the air was rent with a horrific cry, an anguished squeal that was worse than anything I could ever recall hearing.

I flung him back into his cell and the door slammed behind him as I returned to my normal size. I looked to Gavrikov, who stood watching me, impassive. "And you?"

Aleksandr Gavrikov was a difficult man to read at any time. He took a step back, his face falling into shadow that pooled around his mouth and eye sockets, making his expression impossible to gauge. "You are foolish to challenge Sovereign. I will not help you. Not today. Not ever. You are a far cry from the matryoshka I knew so long ago—"

My head whipped around as I flung Gavrikov back into his cell and slammed the door behind him. "And you, Bastian? Are you going to ignore the threat to our kind?"

Bastian stared at me with hard eyes. Duty was everything to him. I knew that. "I don't think I can help you," he said after a long pause.

I felt a swelling of anger like I was going to explode, and just as I started to reach out a hand for him he shook his head. "Let me save you the trouble." He walked back to his box and stepped inside, shutting the door behind him. I raised a hand and locked it with a slashing gesture, purely out of spite.

I turned back to Wolfe, the last of the metas, uncaged. But he was caged, still standing in his box, his shadow staring back at me through the pooling darkness. "What are you going to do, Wolfe? Just sit in the cage until I die, staring at the walls and reliving all your happy memories?" I stepped toward him and still could not see him in the dark.

"Yes," Wolfe said.

"You're just going to sit there?" I asked, incredulous. "Going to sit back and let the guy who pounded the shit out of you in the Forest of Dean—just let him walk away. Just let him kill … every … meta … on the planet? That's what you're gonna do?"

Wolfe's voice was quiet, and all the usual malicious joy was gone from it. "That is all the Wolfe will do … until the end comes.

Until the Little Doll gets broken or killed by Sovereign. Then it will all be over."

"You're a coward," I said with quiet fury.

I could feel him blink, could feel the hostility radiate off of him. His shadow only stirred, but I knew he was tense, ready to spring at me. It was futile, of course. I could hurt him here; he couldn't hurt me. I was in control now.

And he knew it.

His shadow relaxed. "Sovereign will come for the Little Doll eventually, and she is too foolish to heed the Wolfe's advice and run. So if she doesn't play nice with Sovereign, she'll get locked away or he'll wait for another Little Doll to show up. One that *will* play with him. Maybe even your own Little Doll." A chill ran through me. "If the Little Doll ever has one of her own."

"I will … kill him," I said, staring into the abyss of Wolfe's cage. "I will."

A paw extended out far enough to take hold of the door to Wolfe's prison, and it began to shut. "If the Little Doll really believes that … then why is she here?"

He shut the door and I locked it out of habit. The sound echoed, even as I turned back to Zack, who waited behind me.

His face was pale, downcast—and said everything I already knew about my chances of success without the help of my prisoners.

Chapter 5

It was a slow, miserable walk back to the Headquarters building. The sun was rising at my back and I knew it was sure to be another warm late summer's day. I let my hand run over my face, rubbing my brow. There was dirt on my fingers and I could feel it smudge on my forehead as I walked. I didn't care.

I ran my tongue over the roof of my mouth, still tasting the remnants of the coffee I'd had earlier. I'd need more unless I wanted to fall asleep before the day had even begun. Breakfast, too. I felt a little weak, probably from a failure to eat, and my stomach rumbled its assent to my assessment.

There were still figures milling around the construction site where I'd encountered Sovereign. I saw security uniforms, and even a white lab coat that told me Dr. Perugini was there. I took the long way around, dog-legging toward the cafeteria on the back side of the dormitory in order to avoid her. She and I weren't on the best of terms; when I'd talked to her earlier in the night, she was most upset with me for leaving Old Man Winter's burnt corpse to stink up her medical unit.

Winter.

I cursed aloud as I walked, hearing my boots swish through the dewy grass. I'd just had a showdown with the voices in my head, and every last one of them with power had refused to help me. My instincts told me to pound the stuffing out of them, Jack Bauer style, until they gave me what I wanted, but I didn't think I had it in me. Pushing them around and bullying them some was one thing; actively torturing them was another.

I was surprised I drew that line for dead people. They were living rent-free in my head, after all.

I came around the far wing of the dormitory at a fast walk. The enormous glass cube that was the cafeteria sat between the right-angled wings of the building. It was enormous, extending four stories into the air. Even from here, I could smell fresh eggs cooking. My stomach rumbled again. Breakfast would be served soon.

I glanced through the glass windows into the cafeteria and saw figures huddled inside. I recognized a great many of them instantly. They were metas we'd saved from England, mostly. The remnants of Omega. I could smell the pall of fear from outside, too. It wasn't a literal smell, but it was heavier than even the eggs.

I trudged past the cafeteria, keeping my distance. Karthik was inside with them, I knew, along with a few other defenders. Probably Reed by this point. I walked faster, hoping to get around the wing on the other side of the building before I was seen. I wasn't in the mood for conversation.

I sent air rushing through my gritted teeth and thought about Winter again. He'd offered his soul to me, freely, and I'd turned him down. He was a wretched bastard, had killed the only man I'd ever loved by forcing me to touch him. Trying to get me to absorb him for eternity while promising some secret knowledge had seemed like the ultimate revenge, like the last laugh and nastiest dirty trick ever.

If I'd known then what I knew now, I might have taken him up on it.

He had been willing to give me his soul. That meant he might have been willing to show me how to use his power. Not that his power alone would have done me much good, since supposedly Sovereign had righteously beaten and scarred his ass once upon a time, but at least it would have been something.

And I needed something at this point. Actually, to fight Sovereign, I needed a whole lot of something—and that something was power, with a capital P.

I made it around the far wing of the dormitory and saw the main entrance to headquarters. It looked deceptively quiet even though I knew that there were a ton of security personnel standing just inside the lobby with enough firepower to win a small war.

Unfortunately, I was in a bigger war than they were equipped to handle, and I needed all the help I could get.

I made my way across the lawn and stepped onto the sidewalk, following it back to the entry. Every click of my boots against the sidewalk was like a beat of the drum, a cadence as I marched back to my doom.

I had no idea what to do next. I had people to protect that I couldn't really protect. Sovereign had proven that. As if he wasn't bad enough, his second in command, Weissman, could play with time like he carried God's own remote. Pause, fast forward, slow motion, even rewind might have been in his power for all I knew. I'd gotten lucky the last time we fought and caused him a load of pain.

Then I'd gotten all stupid and merciful, letting him get away. I was pretty sure that trying to be the good guy in that situation had caused me to hesitate. I was even more sure it would cost me in the end. Another regret on the pile of them. Another questionable choice in a host of them. They were adding up quicker than I could take inventory.

I breezed through the security checkpoint toward the elevator and hit the button. I was still lost in thought when the doors opened, and I stepped inside without conscious effort.

I was at a dead end. I supposedly had powers, but I didn't know how to use them. I had souls that were supposed to be mine, but were stubbornly refusing to cooperate with me. I had seemingly invincible, unbeatable foes looking down at me like giants staring down at a mouse. Like I'd just looked down on Bjorn.

And they could smash me—and all my people—at will.

I slumped against the back of the elevator car, felt my skull thump against the hard metal, and took a deep breath. What was I supposed to do now? Wait until one of them showed up to kill us all and just throw myself into the fight, hoping that one of my captured souls might decide to help me?

The elevator dinged and started to open before I could compose myself. I could feel the desperation as if it was a passenger in the car with me, holding me tight, suffocating me. I straightened as the doors slid apart to reveal the fourth floor—and someone standing right in the middle of them.

"Sienna," Ariadne said, her face as drawn as I'd ever seen it. "I was just coming to look for you."

"Well, you found me," I said, slapping my sweaty palms against my denim jeans. They felt like they were drenched, just from all that thinking—and dreading. "What's up?"

Ariadne hesitated. Never a good sign. "We just got a call from the Las Vegas Police Department."

I perked up. "Is the extermination starting there?" I paused. The local PD wouldn't call us about something like that; they wouldn't even know who we were or who to call, assuming they had any clue metahumans existed and were operating in their city.

"No," she said, a moment after all that ran through my mind. She paused again, pursing her lips, and I could tell she was having trouble saying what was on her mind. It was almost like she was looking for the best way to phrase it. "They found a body," she said at last. I waited; if Ariadne was seeking me out to tell me this, it had to be important. "It's … someone you know." She bit her lip, toying with the edge of it. "They think it's your Aunt Charlie."

Chapter 6

The knock sounded at my door as I was finishing packing. "Who is it?" I asked as I carried my overnight bag into the living room and set it down next to the table.

"It's me." My mother's voice came muffled through the door. "Let me in."

"If that's not a metaphor for our relationship, I don't know what is," I said, my bare feet sinking into the tall pile of my carpeting. "You demand something, I immediately have to answer it." My hand gripped the metal handle slickly; my palms were still sweaty. I opened the door.

She was standing there with her dark hair still wound in a tight ponytail, her sharp jaw line protruding, arms folded. It was totally a mother thing to do—except she was standing in such a way that I could have knocked her flat on her ass with one good punch. That wasn't really like her.

"You heard?" I asked.

"I heard." She kept her arms folded as she stepped into my room. "You're going out there?"

"To identify the body, yes." I closed the door behind her. She took care to avoid me as she passed. I was wearing gym shorts and a short-sleeved t-shirt while she was still rocking a leather jacket and jeans on a summer's day. Her one concession to the heat of Minnesota summer seemed to be her lack of gloves, but she kept her hands tucked safely under her arms, so she wasn't exactly living dangerously. "Someone has to."

"I could go," she said stiffly.

"You could," I agreed, making my way back to my bag. I checked the zippers absently, fiddling with them even though I remembered closing them before I'd moved it out of my bedroom. "But I figured I'd do this myself."

We basked in the silence for a moment before she had to go and ruin it. "You're running away."

I didn't yell, I didn't scream, I didn't throw anything at her or grab hold of her until her soul came ripping out of her body. Though I was mightily tempted on all four of those counts. "I'm going to identify your sister's body in Las Vegas and then I'll be right back."

"You're scared."

I pushed my lips together in a tight smile. "I'm not the one who's probably going to die. He wants me alive, after all. What do I have to worry about?" Other than being the concubine of a genocidal maniac.

"You're scared of what's going to happen if you fail." She did not look amused. "You think he'll—"

"I don't think *he'll* do anything," I said. "I think Weissman, lovely and caring soul that he is, will take that knife of his to everyone around here with all of his trademark enthusiasm and charm. I think everyone here will die screaming if I don't find a way to stop him, which—hey, surprise—I don't have one." I felt my whole body cry out to do something, to move, to vent frustration in some direction, but I held it back. "I've got nothing. No solution. No special powers. Nada." I held my hands up to reveal how empty they were and shrugged my shoulders as though that simple gesture could relieve them of the weight of all the people who were looking to me to save them.

"You can't run," she said. She looked like she was hugging herself, like she was gripping herself tight to keep from—I don't know—slugging me, probably.

"I'll be back tomorrow," I said. "I doubt Weissman will move in tonight."

"And if he does?" She almost sounded like her voice was going to quiver. Almost.

I let my head sink down until I was staring at the floor, examining the carpet fibers. “Then I guess he’ll get one less piece of cannon fodder than he planned for.”

I listened to her taking slow breaths for a long moment before she finally turned on her heel and walked out the door.

Chapter 7

I was dressed a little more professionally when I got on the plane to Vegas. I wore a suit jacket with my jeans and slung my bag over my shoulder. I never was much of a purse girl, and it was probably never more obvious than now, as I sat in the first-class section in the large seat, the dull thrum of the overhead vents fading into the background chatter of the coach passengers loading behind us.

I'd only flown commercial airlines a few times. The one that stuck out most in my memory was my trip to London and back. It had been the sort of rough hell that I wouldn't wish on many people: a nine-hour flight each way that rendered me cramped and annoyed, vowing to never get on an airplane again.

Yet here I was, this time for a three-hour flight which I would reprise tomorrow. All so I could go look at a corpse and make sure it was my aunt's. I let out a long sigh, the stale, stuffy, filtered smell of the plane's air conditioning running through my nose.

I'd seen enough corpses to last eight lifetimes, and I was only nineteen years old.

I thought again about what my mother said, about how I was running away. I didn't really want to admit it, but she was right. She was dead on. Maybe not correct in her reasoning, but correct in the symptom.

It wasn't like I was afraid to die. I'd rather have died than go on with all the people I cared about back at the campus dead.

No, I was afraid of the future. I didn't even want to think about it. Unfortunately, my brain didn't share those feelings, because it had put this thought on a loop in my mind.

I didn't think Weissman would be coming immediately.

Something about the way Sovereign—Joshua—whatever his name was—talked about the whole thing made me think Weissman had other stuff to do before he came for us.

Of course, I'd still feel like holy hell if he got there while I was gone.

I took another breath of the synthetic-smelling, recirculated air, listening to the man in front of me talking with the stewardess as she took his coat and offered him a glass of something alcoholic. I had already decided to pass on that if it came my way. Not because I was underage, but because this business I was heading to Las Vegas to attend to was grim and worthy of seriousness. Not drunkenness. No matter how great the temptation might have been to be hammered.

I hadn't seen my Aunt Charlie in a year or so. Not since she'd saved me from that asshole James Fries then proceeded to beat the hell out of me herself. My mother had saved me on that one and threatened Charlie so strongly that we'd caught not a whiff of her heavily perfumed ass since. Even the Agency sources had drawn a blank on her when I'd had them snoop around a few months ago.

It was like she'd disappeared. Which was probably for the best.

And now she was dead.

Another guy in a suit appeared in the aisle as I kept my head down, staring at the seatback in front of me. It was in its upright and locked position, like it was supposed to be. Not that it mattered, I supposed. Here in first class, there was actually a decent space between me and the next seat. I was short enough I never had a problem with the leg room, but I could certainly tell the difference.

"Is this seat taken?" The guy in the suit asked, drawing my attention. I wasn't sure at first if he was legitimately asking me or if he was just bantering with the stewardess. I turned to look at him and immediately resisted the urge to throw a backhand out to smack him.

"You ass," I said. "What are you doing here?"

"Following you," Scott said as he sat down in the seat next to me, his pressed, pristine white shirt unbuttoned at the top in what looked like—to me—another expression of his slightly cocky, preppy, pretty-boy charm. He leaned on the armrest between us and smiled. "Figured you might need some help."

"I'm identifying the body of someone you've never really met," I said. "What do you think I'll be needing your help with?"

"I'd say emotional support," he said, still smiling, "but I'm a little worried you don't have any emotions right now." It was a little charming. Just a little.

"Oh, I have them," I said, leaning toward the window. "Nice to know I'm keeping them beneath the surface, though. I'd hate to be bleeding them all over everyone right now."

"You are the leader," he said. "All eyes are on you. I'd imagine that's difficult."

"It can be." The little circular vent above me started hissing air at a higher volume, and it felt cooler than it had a moment ago. The light thrum of the plane's electrical systems changed into something heavier as the engines started up. "Look … if this is about you and me—"

"It's not," he said, still leaning toward me. There wasn't just a simple arm-rest like I'd dealt with in coach; there was a full-on end-table-sized surface between the two of us. "I told you, I don't need an answer from you on that, not until after. But—you are walking into something right now that you shouldn't have to face alone. You ought to have someone there with you when you—"

"Charlie's not exactly a fond memory for me, okay?" I cut him off, but I did it quietly. "It's not like I spent my childhood playing at her house, or had her with me during the toughest times of my life. I knew her for six months before she tried to kill me. Six months during which I'd see her for a day a month when she was blowing through town. I don't think that Charlie dying and me having to look at her corpse is going to be something that sends me over the edge emotionally."

"Well, I'm here for you anyway," Scott said, and he pulled back from me a little. Still kept on that charming smile, though. "Even if all you need is someone to drive the rental car."

"What if I want to drive the rental car?"

His smile evaporated. "You're kidding, right? I always drive."

"Unless you're too drunk to do so," I said with a little smile of my own.

"Yeah, but that's not going to happen here." He actually scoffed. I almost couldn't believe it.

"Scott, we're going to Vegas," I said. "With government-issued IDs that say we're over twenty-one. You can't tell me that these thoughts have not occurred to you before stepping onto this plane."

He shook his head and pursed his lips into a thin line. "I'm a little insulted that you think so little of me—" He snickered. "Okay, maybe—just maybe—I'll concede that it crossed my mind that you needed to find a way to leave behind some of that emotional baggage that's weighing you down. Even for just a night."

I looked out the window as the tarmac started to move. White concrete lit by the hot, noonday sun shimmered outside my window. "I don't think a night's gonna do it. We're staring at the end of the world as we know it here, Scott." I glanced back at him and caught him looking at me, face all filled with concern. "Whatever baggage I might try to leave behind, I have to pick right back up when I reach my destination."

"You got the weight of the world on you right now, Sienna." He leaned closer again, and I caught the light scent of his cologne. It wasn't bad anymore; just enough to give me a pleasant whiff. "It wouldn't hurt to let all that go for one night. Just one night. And then—like you said—you can just pick it right back up tomorrow.

Who knows? Maybe a night of rest will make it feel a little lighter, or give you an idea for a new way to carry it—" He broke off. "My metaphor is falling apart."

I arched my eyebrows, but I know my face kept its regular grimness. I lightly chewed on my bottom lip. "What if it's heavier when I pick it back up? You know, like when you've had a good workout, and you max yourself out and—"

"I told you, the metaphor didn't work," he said. "You need distance. You need perspective. You need a mental break. It's been months of grinding up against jagged edges—"

"That sounds like something dirty that you'd do to a metal band," I said with a frown.

"Just … trust me?" Scott said. "A little break. Something to get your mind off things. Refocus, recharge."

"I'll … think about it," I said as we started to taxi. A voice came on after a dinging sound, the flight attendant starting to announce our departure. The safety instructions started on a video screen overhead as I stared at the back of the seat in front of me.

"That's all I ask," Scott said. "Just some thought."

We settled into silence as the safety instructions went on and I tuned them out. They passed in both an eyeblink and yet torturously slowly, somehow simultaneously. Once they were finished, I felt the plane throttle up to high speed and the nose came up, pushing me lightly against the back of the seat.

A few seconds later I felt us leave the ground, a weightless sensation that felt like it applied only to me. And for that moment, it almost seemed like I could leave all those problems that had been weighing me down behind me on the ground.

Chapter 8

The morgue smelled like death. The air was freezing cold as it poured out of the overhead ducts, the interior ceiling of the place looking like one of those warehouse-chic restaurants with the exposed vents and whatnot. The rest of the morgue was done in cool colors, mostly blue tones with stainless steel.

The medical examiner was a woman, and she was bored. I could tell by way she was playing a game on her iPhone, popping her gum like one of those annoying secretaries in an eighties movie. She stopped when we walked in, and I noticed as the pink bubble deflated between her lips that she had a little stud just above her chin and a couple of piercings in each eyebrow. Her hair was a wicked red that clashed with the gum.

"Can I help you?" She put on a smile for us, and it wasn't blatantly fake. More cool, professional. She looked like she might have been my age, actually.

"Yeah," I said, and flashed her my badge. The best thing about it was that I was cleared to carry my gun on airplanes, so I hadn't had to worry about picking up my pistol and reloading it after the flight at the baggage claim; I just grabbed my carry-on and went. "I'm here to identify a body."

"Hmmm, I'm gonna guess Charlene Nealon," she said, and the gum disappeared into the back of her mouth. "Did you sign in at the front desk?"

"Yeah," I said, and glanced at the double doors leading into the next room.

She stood and revealed a band t-shirt under her white lab coat, which was immaculate. "I'm Lauren, by the way. Follow me."

Scott gave me a look that showed his surprise at the slightly unconventional medical examiner we were dealing with, but we followed.

"They found her under the footbridge that leads from Treasure Island to the mall," Lauren said, like I should know where that was. She didn't go too fast—not that she could have outwalked two metas—but she didn't look back to see if we were behind her, either. She brushed through the double doors and the smell of the morgue got heavier. I didn't gag, but I felt the urge. "Skull was busted open, bruising around her throat like she'd been throttled. Laceration on her abdomen." She glanced back at me. "It's not pretty. I've seen worse, but it's not going to be for the weak of stomach."

I bristled a little that she didn't look at Scott as she said it. "I've seen dead bodies before, thanks."

"Just giving you a warning," she said with a shrug then looked to Scott. "You too. If you give me a couple minutes, I could put a sheet around the back of her head so you don't have to see the—"

"It's fine," I said, a little tense. "We can handle it."

"If you say so." Her eyes flared in a way that told me—when coupled with her tone—she thought we were both going to be dry-heaving on her floor in a matter of moments. She led us over to a wall of stainless steel drawers and scanned for a second until she found the one she was looking for. She slid it open and then pulled the table out with nothing more than a squeal. The outline of a body was visible beneath a white sheet. "So, are you here just to identify? Because generally I don't get FBI agents from Minneapolis in here to check out local homicide vics."

"She's my aunt," I said, glancing at Lauren. "I'll need to know some details on—"

"I can give you the report," Lauren said. Her tone was muted, as if it was her way of being sympathetic for my loss. "No toxicology results yet, though, and the forensics will be a few days."

"We can expedite that," Scott said. Though I'm sure he was

trying to be helpful, I saw Lauren blanch subtly at that, and watched her expression harden. Probably a territorial thing.

"Okay," she said, indifferent. "Here she is." Her fingers were clenched around the top of the sheet. "You sure you want to see her in all her gory glory? I cleaned her up, but she died of massive blunt force trauma to the skull and there's only so much—"

"Just show me," I said. She did, lifting the sheet and folding it back under Charlie's collarbones.

And it was Charlie; that much there wasn't any doubt about. I tried to keep my eyes on her face, stopping them from looking any farther down than her ears. Her head rested low on the steel table, impossibly, unnaturally low for any normal person who had a fully-formed skull. It was blatantly obvious even without doing anything more than glancing that Charlie no longer had a fully-formed skull, though. At least the back half was missing, maybe more.

I looked away from her and ran my tongue up, inadvertently making a clicking noise against the back of my teeth. It felt horribly inappropriate given the circumstances. "Did they … uh … did her killer … take the back of her … uh …" The smell of death, of rot and stink, filled my nose. It was almost overwhelming.

"The back of her skull? Nope," Lauren said and, unprompted, covered Charlie back up. I watched my aunt's blank, pallid face disappear beneath a sheet of white that was only a few shades off from the same tone as her flesh. Considering how tanned and vibrant Charlie had been in life, it was a dramatic change. "Not sure how much you want to know, but we have the pieces of it—and her brains. They're all accounted for, just not—ummm—I couldn't put her back together. That's really more a mortician's area of expertise." She looked a little abashed at this admission.

"Good God," Scott breathed from next to me. I didn't look at him because I didn't want to see if he was affected the way I was.

"Have you had any other bodies come through like this?" It was the only thing that came to my mind. I kept my eyes anchored on Lauren, refusing to even look at the sheet that covered the body.

"Nope," Lauren said as she slid the body back into the drawer and locked it. "Lots of homicides lately, but nothing like this. You see this kind of thing in high-speed car accidents or in suicides, if they jump from really high. Saw a guy one time that got murdered with a candlestick across the back of his head. Like Colonel Mustard got him in the drawing room or something. It did some nasty damage. But someone slammed into a wall like this? Nah. Whoever did it had to be hella strong."

I put my hands over my face, rubbing my skin, not caring what Lauren thought of me at this point. "And the bruising around the neck?"

"Happened before death," she said. "She was probably hanging by the neck for a little bit. Usually if there's bruising happening at the time of death or near it, contusions don't form. By her bruising, someone had her good and tight before she got her head caved in. It might have even resulted in her death absent the trauma to her skull."

I looked at the morgue drawer, the stainless steel glowering back at me in the faint glare of the fluorescent lights. I could see the outline of the three of us staring at it. I had no love lost for Charlie, but she hadn't deserved to die like this.

"You want that postmortem report?" Lauren asked, and she popped her gum so absently I doubted she even knew she did it.

"Yeah," I said, turning away from the drawer my aunt was lying dead inside, missing half her skull. "Why don't you get that for us?"

"Sure," she said, and looked back at us as she turned to leave. "I'm afraid I have to ask you to come with me. I can't leave anyone alone in here."

"Why not?" Scott asked with a note of amusement that was

belied by how waxy he looked. His usually ruddy complexion was ashen. “They’re already dead.”

“Exactly,” Lauren said, like that explained everything. “Necrophiliacs are everywhere.”

There was a moment of silence after that. “You’re joking, right?” Scott asked, his jaw hanging loose.

Lauren shrugged like it didn’t matter. “Follow me, please.”

“Come on,” Scott said, and he put his hand on my shoulder to steer me out. I wasn’t exactly having trouble getting going under my own power, but it felt good anyway. I let him guide me gently along, a comforting weight that was different than the one that was on my shoulders the rest of the time—the weight of responsibility.

Chapter 9

I read the autopsy report while Scott drove us to our hotel. Our rental was a mid-sized SUV, which Scott kept reasonably steady save for when some maniac cab driver cut in front of us with inches to spare before a traffic light. Scott let fly an obscene gesture and then a helpful dose of profanity that caused me to look up at him for a moment before I returned to my reading. The AC was blowing full power and the dashboard thermometer told us it was over a hundred degrees outside.

"Anything interesting?" He eased the car into a gentle turn onto a boulevard marked Spring Mountain Road. He was following the GPS on his phone, which was resting in the cup holder in the black plastic center console between us.

"Not much more than she already told us," I said, thumbing to the last page and skimming. When I was done, I shut the thin booklet. "It kept telling me to refer to the enclosed pictures while describing the wreckage of her body, but thankfully she left those out."

Scott grunted and didn't say anything. The buildings were growing taller around us, casino towers sticking high into the air, impressive facades with more industrial-looking buildings behind them. There was minimal foot traffic here, just a few people now and again who looked like casino employees heading toward bus stops after their shifts.

I could see the Las Vegas Strip ahead of us, a grey stone footbridge at the corner of Las Vegas Boulevard crossing over the street ahead. It was slanted diagonally away from us, toward the mall. Palm trees lined either side of the road and the mall's facade was a square-tiled oddity that just looked out of place.

The crowds grew thicker as we drew closer to the strip. As we approached the footbridge, I sent Scott a look that made clear my expectations. I wondered if he'd see it the same way as he slowed the car down and pulled off to the side of the road. I guess he had.

I opened the door and stepped out into the sweltering heat. I felt like my body had been balled up and shoved into an oven. The air was dry, so dry I felt like I couldn't even sweat at first. I stood there, half-wishing I could climb back into the sweet, cool SUV before I slammed the door, sealing my decision behind me.

There was a cop standing next to the yellow tape that surrounded the crime scene. I didn't see a cruiser anywhere in sight, and I wondered how long this poor bastard had been standing out here in this hell. I flashed my badge at him and he nodded as I ducked low under the tape.

"Howdy," he said, thumbs in his belt like an aw-shucks cowboy or something. He was wearing a khaki cop uniform, with black shades that made him look super-cool. He even had a crew-cut haircut that made him look like he'd just gotten out of the military.

"Officer Nash," I said, reading his badge from a little ways away. I saw his eyebrows move up in surprise that I called him by his name. "I'm Agent Nealon, this is Agent Byerly. FBI."

"Ma'am," he said, deferring enough that I caught a whiff of ex-military from him. I wondered if he'd served overseas; if he had, this slightly-above-one-hundred-degrees heat was probably like a warm bath to him compared to Iraq or Afghanistan.

"They got you standing out here all day?" I asked. The crime scene tape had been stretched around a splotchy break in the wall beneath the overpass where skull had met concrete, and both had yielded some before concrete won the battle.

"Just a couple hours of my shift, ma'am," he said, and I glanced back to see him at attention, hands off his belt. "They wouldn't leave anyone out here all day, but we had a request from your Agent Li to keep it cordoned off until you'd had a chance to look around."

"Did you?" I hadn't known Li had done that. I was a little surprised, actually; he and I didn't really get along that well.

"Yes, ma'am," Nash said, all business.

"Well, I'm here now," I said, staring at that spot on the wall. "So you can go."

I sensed his hesitation without even looking. "Are you sure, ma'am? If you'd like, I could—"

"It's fine," I said. I stared at the dark markings where dried blood—and other organic residue—caked the spot where the wall had cracked. It had shattered outward in a roughly circular pattern, and I imagined Charlie pinned against it like it was her own version of a halo. "Get yourself some water."

"Yes, ma'am," Officer Nash said and retreated. His steps were precise, a military cadence, as he walked back toward the escalator that led up the footbridge. I lost sight of him as he went up.

"Why are we here?" Scott said from behind me as I stared again at the broken wall where my aunt had had her brains splattered. "We're not detectives, Sienna. We're not criminologists. There's not a lot of hope we're going to connect the dots and solve this murder."

"How do you know?" I asked, staring at the place where Charlie's life had ended. Unexpectedly. Abruptly. "The report said it looked like she'd run after being lacerated on the abdomen." I stared at the people moving along the strip ahead. "Shouldn't there be surveillance camera footage?" I cursed the fact that I'd sent Officer Nash on his merry way before asking.

"This has got to be one of the most heavily trafficked roadways in the US," Scott said. "You'd think there'd be something."

"Why cut her and then bludgeon her?" I asked. I looked back from the strip to the broken wall. "Totally overmatched her, lifted her off her feet—that has to be a meta."

"Well, she was a meta," Scott said, "so wouldn't it make sense if she was running with a meta crowd?"

"That wasn't Charlie's style," I said, and I looked around absently as I felt the beads of sweat start on my upper lip. "She liked to be the toughest one in the room; it gave her an advantage. She preyed on weakness, she didn't admire strength." I looked at her splatter marks, and realized the blood had sprayed outward in its own circular pattern. "When she was overmatched, she'd run. So she got cut and she ran. But they caught her and killed her anyway." I tapped my fingers against my chin. "Is it possible …?" I let my voice trail off.

"You're thinking she got caught up in the extinction?" Scott asked.

"That medical examiner said they'd been busy lately," I said and wiped the sweat off my upper lip. The heat was starting to make my back itch, but there wasn't much I could do about that at the moment.

"Look at you, following up on leads and suggesting patterns," Scott said, "like a regular Sherlock."

"Sherlock would already have it figured out by now," I said and finally turned away from the wall. I couldn't look at it anymore. My face melted into a cringe. I wasn't close to tears, but the sight of it … hurt, for some reason. Sickened me.

"Come on," Scott said, and put his hand on my shoulder again. I started back toward the car and he walked beside me. "I'll call the LVMPD and see if I can track down some video for this … this …" He was lost for words.

"Call it what it is," I said as I shrugged his hand off my shoulder when we broke at the car; I headed to my side and he to the driver's. "It was a slaughter. Pure and simple." I glanced back one last time at the bloody, broken wall where my aunt had been crowned into the afterlife. "Whoever did this, Charlie never stood a chance against them."

Chapter 10

We were sharing a suite at the Palazzo, which was not as awkward as it sounded. Scott, because he was a gentleman (or possibly because he feared death), had volunteered to sleep on the couch. I was undecided about whether I would take him up on that or let him sleep in the bed. If he'd worn as much cologne as he used to, it would have been the couch for sure. Now that he'd learned some moderation, I was torn.

We'd stowed our baggage and nipped downstairs to the Palazzo's promenade for dinner at a steakhouse that looked entirely too fancy. They didn't balk at the fact I was wearing jeans under my blazer, though, and I didn't balk when they handed me a menu that included a rib eye that cost more than fifty dollars.

I did, however, consider putting the menu down and leaving. But I didn't. Because it wasn't like I couldn't pay for it out of my own pocket if I needed to. I didn't spend money on anything else, and my housing was paid for, after all.

"Nice of the Agency to splurge for dinner," Scott said with a smile, glancing over the leather-bound menu. His voice made him sound pensive, but I suspect he was closer to drooling. We hadn't had lunch, and it was close to seven o'clock our time. "Living first class on the taxpayer's dime."

"We've never gotten a cent of taxpayer money," I said, probably a little defensively. As putative head of the Agency, it was probably my responsibility to defend budgetary decisions. Which we didn't really worry about, since Congress never asked about our budget and we never asked them for money. "Ariadne didn't say anything about a budget for this trip, so …"

Scott smiled as he looked up from behind the menu. "I bet she won't make that mistake again. Ariadne tends to watch the dollars and cents."

"She's never fought me on anything," I said, pretty settled on that rib eye. I was trying to figure out how a steak could be worth fifty dollars. And I'd had some pretty good steaks before. "Is this steak really fifty bucks?"

Scott looked back at the menu. "Yes."

I closed the leather volume in front of me. "And it's a piece of meat?"

He cocked his head at me, eyes filled with curiosity. "Yes ..."

There was a low-hanging light above our table and I leaned across, under it, my shadow darkening the unsullied white tablecloth. "It's not like ... magical meta steak that has powers beyond those of a regular steak? Able to—I don't know? Cure cancer for the eater? Give them off-the-charts sex appeal that will allow them to sleep with anyone?"

"No," Scott said, and he seemed amused. "Well, maybe on the sex appeal. It's just a steak, albeit probably a very good one. Haven't you ever eaten at a fancy restaurant before?"

"I used to go to Biaggi's sometimes in Eden Prairie Center," I said, thinking about the Italian place that Zack and I had gone to. I felt a pang of embarrassment thinking of Zack locked up in my head right now, probably watching this whole scene play out in ... well, dismay. Or horror. Something. "I used to love Santorini's, but I'm pretty sure their steaks topped out at about thirty dollars or so." I had also gone there with Zack. My cheeks burned with embarrassment, but I didn't dare check on him, not now.

"We should go to Manny's in Minneapolis some time," Scott said. There was a gleam in his eye as he spoke. "Or Pittsburgh Blue. They've both got steaks for fifty dollars."

"I haven't even gotten over eating one steak for fifty dollars and you're already trying to talk me into two more?" I glanced back at the menu and then shut it. The price was not going to fall anytime soon simply by me staring at it in disbelief. "That's ballsy."

"Confident," Scott corrected.

I looked at him as I put the menu down. "I admire your optimism, but it might just be unfounded. I don't see myself going out for a lot of fancy dinners once we get back to Minneapolis and I—as you put it—pick up my baggage."

"This problem won't last forever," Scott said with a light shrug as he matched my movement and put his menu down as well. The black leather binder stood out on the white tablecloth. "You're going to figure out how to use your powers, and we're gonna beat Sovereign and Century like they're a cheap steak and we're a tenderizing hammer." He paused. "See what I did there? What with us being in an expensive steakhouse and all—"

"Subtle." I cut him off, letting my fingers hold up my face as I leaned on my elbow, staring at him. "Listen … I don't know what you think is going to happen, but I—" I glanced around. There was no sign of our waiter, for which I was actually grateful, in spite of being hungry enough to order the uncooked, unskinned hindquarters of the cow if it were available now. "I think your faith in me might be unfounded."

"You'll get it," he said and waved a hand at me in utter dismissal. "I'm surprised you haven't gotten it yet, I mean—"

"I don't know how to do it," I said, brutally cutting him off. "I've tried. I dug deep, talked to my little collection of matryoshkas within, and—it doesn't work. No chance. Nothing. They're not even talking to me at this point." I leaned back in my chair, feeling like I'd achieved some mighty victory by throwing this desperate, horrible information at Scott right in the middle of a restaurant so fancy I wasn't sure even my most expensive clothes belonged here.

"Hello, my name is Garion, and I'll be your server tonight," a shorter man said as he approached us with a little flourish. His uniform was natty-neat and matched with everything else I'd seen in the restaurant thus far. "Sorry for the delay, but I can get you started with anything?"

I didn't answer at first and neither did Scott, each of us staring at the other across the table. Finally, I did speak. "Just water for me."

"The same," Scott said, and his voice scratched in his throat like he'd drunk a bottle of sand straight out of the desert.

"Let me tell you about our specials for the night," Gar said, but I was already tuning him out. My eyes were fixed on Scott. His face was red, eyes downcast, hands folded in front of him. I watched him as the waiter talked on, without a reaction from either of us, and knew that I'd thrown the entire weight of my baggage on him.

And just as it had done to me, it completely crushed him under its weight.

Chapter 11

When I awoke, it took me a minute to get my bearings. I was wrapped in soft cloth sheets pressing against my exposed shoulders and arms. I could feel the lines of my tank top and sweatpants because sleeping in anything was so foreign to me. I adjusted my body as I sat up, the sunlight flooding in from the massive windows that took up an entire wall.

The city of Las Vegas was spread out before me, hotels on the other side of the road obstructing my view only a little. There were mountains in the distance, dust-covered and plain, so unlike the green, verdant and snow-capped ones I had seen on TV. I stared out at the vista, all that wide-open space, and took a long breath.

Between the window and the bed was a sitting area filled with ugly green-tinted couches that had a dark pattern embroidered on the cloth. The scent of Scott's cologne was the only thing in the air, and fortunately it was faint. I could see the top of his head over the small wall separating the bed from the sitting area. His gaze was tilted down, focused on the glass-top coffee table in front of him.

I yawned and clapped a hand over my mouth. I had dragon breath, no doubt, and suspected that his meta senses would allow him to detect it even from ten feet away. That was one of the drawbacks to the enhanced senses of a meta; I'd learned to ignore it somewhat after months of kissing Zack and tasting the hints of whatever he'd most recently eaten. I'd also bugged him about breath mints and brushing his teeth more often, the poor guy.

"You're awake," Scott said without turning to face me.

"Naw," I replied, "I'm just sleepwalking, that's all. Ignore me, and eventually I'll pitch over and start snoring again." He laughed nervously, but still did not turn to face me. "Oh, God, I don't snore, do I?"

"What?" He finally turned his head around, and I saw him from the cheeks up, the rest of him blocked by the short partition wall between me and the sitting area. "No, I didn't hear any snoring. I think you laughed at one point, kind of softly."

I put my back against the wooden headboard and pulled my knees to my chest, letting my hands slide down the soft fabric of my sweatpants. "I find it hard to believe I'd have anything to laugh about in my dreams."

"Maybe I was dreaming, then," Scott said with a shrug. "I contacted the local PD about the surveillance cameras on the strip when your aunt was killed. They have nothing."

"How is that possible?" I climbed out of bed, felt my face burn with the heat of shock as the blankets fell away from me.

"They don't know," Scott said. "The recordings are just missing, like someone came in and stole them. You're talking about multiple casinos, multiple security rooms. Not one of them has a recording, not on either side of the street during that time. That also includes the local PD's cameras. It's a professional job of some sort, though it's totally baffling them how anyone could just erase every recording without anyone seeing them do it."

"Weissman," I said, jumping to the conclusion before I even knew I was doing it. "It has to be Weissman."

"That guy you ran into in England?" Scott was frowning now. "How do you know?"

"He probably froze time and just went in to each of the security rooms," I said and started to stretch. I made a noise with my mouth as I vented air. "Think about it: unless someone could magically—or meta-poweredly—go invisible and sneak in there to delete the recordings—because I presume they're digital?" I waited for his nod to go on. "So, yeah, someone went in and deleted them without making a fuss. Ergo, Weissman."

"He can do that?" Scott scratched his face, and I noticed a five o'clock shadow on his cheeks, upper lip and chin.

"Yeah, he's a real Barry Allen-type," I said.

Scott's face creased in a frown. "He sings 'Copacabana'?"

I rolled my eyes. "Barry Allen is the Flash. Barry Manilow sings 'Copacabana.'"

"Ahh," Scott said, his face relaxing. "I was wondering what Lola being a showgirl had to do with deleting recordings."

I ignored him. "This doesn't do us any good, though. Assuming it was Weissman behind the killing doesn't tell us much, except that I guess it relates to the extermination."

"Unless it was someone else with Weissman's powers," Scott said. "Is there anyone else with his powers?"

"Someone named Akiyama," I said, with a frown of my own. "I think. Weissman talked about some guy who had his powers but with more ability. Wolfe gave me the name." I racked my brain, calling out into the darkened rooms at the back, but no answer came from Wolfe to confirm it.

"Listen," Scott said, and I could hear a cool urgency in his tone, "I've been thinking about this whole situation. I don't think it's as bad as you're assuming it is."

"So … our entire species isn't being wiped out systematically by the most powerful meta in the world and his hundred sidekicks?" I stretched while I said it, like it was totally minor, a distraction in my otherwise aimless day.

"Oh, no, it totally is," Scott said, with a little more enthusiasm than I would have had in his shoes, "I just think you're over-worrying."

I sat there in dumb silence for a moment. "Thousands of people are dying, we're heading toward the twilight of metakind, humanity is probably going to be under an uber-powerful maniac's boot afterward … and you think I'm OVER-worrying?" I stood there and pursed my lips. "I'm sitting in Las Vegas investigating the murder of an aunt who tried to kill me when last we met instead of protecting the people I vowed to guard. I'm not sure your analysis is …" I let my voice trail off rather than say something flagrantly insulting to him, "… entirely rational."

"I'm just saying that I think you can overcome this," Scott said. He gave me a smile that was probably supposed to be heartening, but wasn't.

"They hate me, Scott," I said, not flinching away from him. "Hate me."

His face crumpled into a puzzled frown. "You mean … the people at Agency?"

I suspect my face turned slightly scathing but then loosened. "Them too, for all I know. But I was talking about the voices in my head. You know, the source of these superpowers I'm supposed to be able to call upon? They hate me."

"Well, you can fix that—"

"I can't fix that, Scott," I made a sound that was semi-amused, a mirthless laugh. "Don't you get it? I've never been sweet, just mean. I'm the mean girl. My personality is razor wire drenched in lemon juice. I was raised with a sword in my hand and nary a kind thought in my head. I'm cut off from humanity—mine and everyone else's. My first instinct is to be snarky and shitty to people, and most of the time I suck at reining in that instinct. The voices in my head are confined in metal boxes in my mind because I didn't like hearing them. I couldn't deal with having their thoughts and conversations blotting out my ability to function, so I shut them up by throwing them into captivity. And they hate me for it. Whatever Sovereign's got going on with his soul captives, it's not like the relationship I have with mine. I'm their jailer, not their friend, and they won't help me even if we're about to die, because what I'm doing to them on a daily basis is worse than death."

Scott's face was blank, ashen. "You could … try letting them out?"

I wanted to snap at him, but I couldn't. "I tried. Sort of. I don't know. It's not looking good."

He took a deep breath. "Well … okay."

"Okay?" I looked at him in disbelief. "I don't think any of this is okay, but …"

"I mean it's not good, obviously," Scott said, holding up his hands in a gesture of utter surrender that told me he didn't want to argue with me. "But, uh … you know, we have a little more time."

"We have *some* time," I said. "But I don't know how much."

"Seems like we're pretty much at a dead end with this Charlie investigation," he said. "What do you want to do?"

I sagged back onto the bed, felt my rump hit it and sink into the soft mattress. "I don't know. I don't know what else to do." I fell back and let myself lie there, staring up at the ceiling. "But I don't want to go home yet." That much I was certain of. It was like home was an opposite-pole magnet to me, the very thought of getting on a plane to go back repelling me.

Scott was quiet for a moment, and then I heard him dial his cell phone, the odd, atonal notes causing me to crane my neck to look over at him. He held the phone up to his ear, and I watched him turn toward the window. The sun shone through, the sky a light azure. I wondered how long I'd slept; it'd felt like forever.

"Ariadne?" Scott's voice jarred me out of a trance. "I need the file on that wildfire meta that killed someone out here in Vegas a few weeks ago." He paused, and I could hear a faint voice talking on the other end of the line. "We're waiting for something from the local PD, figured we'd poke around while we're killing time." He paused and looked back at me. "It's going good. We'll be back soon—just figured we'd …" He smiled at me, "… kill two birds with one stone."

Chapter 12

I stepped out of the car into the Vegas summer heat and immediately started to sweat. The hot air wrapped me up like a blanket, curling around my body and making me want to hang my tongue out like a dog. And then spray it with water. From a fire hose. On full blast. I don't know, I think the heat was messing with my mind.

It felt like the soles of my shoes were melting off as I walked over the black asphalt pavement toward the pawnshop. Every step was a dragging misery, the smell of nearby Tropicana Avenue's smoggy traffic making me want to wave a hand in front of my face to clear my nose. The greasy breakfast buffet we'd hit on the way to the pawnshop where the murder had occurred was lodged in the back of my throat. Should have spent the extra money and eaten at the hotel.

Scott rushed ahead to open the door for me. He already had a bead of sweat running down his temple. I envied him in that regard, though I doubt it made him feel any cooler.

The rush of the air conditioning in the pawnshop was inadequate yet still blissful after the walk from the car. Cool air ran over my body, lifting the blanket of heat that had wrapped itself around me. I adjusted my suit jacket in something that probably looked like the Picard maneuver as I surveyed the green-carpeted, wood-paneled room that held more broken dreams than a Taylor Swift song.

Guitars were everywhere up front. Wooden, acoustic, whatever. Enough musical instruments to equip a band large enough to play behind Sinatra himself were lining the shelves in front of me. I studied them with a kind of distaste. People sold them for various reasons, I'd guess, but I suspected the most frequent one involved lack of money and giving up a dream. Don't think you're going to be a professional guitar player anytime soon? Might as well turn that old Fender into cash, right? I wondered disdainfully how much of it ended up in a casino slot machine.

"You're, uh … kind of scowling," Scott whispered to me.

"So?" I softened my tone a little.

"It's not the best image to project when we're here to get info," Scott said. "You're gonna scare people."

"I'm a nineteen year-old girl—woman—glaring at the musical instruments in a pawnshop with a sour look on her face," I said. "Anyone watching is probably just going to think I dated a musician who was an asshole."

"Come on," Scott said, and now he was scowling.

We approached the glass counter that circled the room. A twenty-something guy was standing behind it, medium height, medium build. I waited for him to speak and wondered if I'd find him medium annoying. At this point, I'd take it, honestly. Better than highly annoying.

"Can I help you?" His voice came out way too cheery, way too smarmy, and way too high for his frame. I buried my disappointment in a low sigh that caused Scott to send me a searing glare.

"Scott Byerly, FBI," he said and flipped his badge open.

"Whoa," Medium-to-Annoying-Guy said. His name tag helpfully read Samuel, but he was destined to always be Medium-to-Annoying-Guy to me. Wait. Who goes by Samuel instead of Sam? I dropped the Medium from his title. "What … uh … can I help you with?"

"The robbery," I said, cutting to the chase before Annoying Samuel got too far on my already frayed nerves. "Were you here that day?"

"Yeah," Samuel said with a quick nod. He was heavily freckled and his hair was stubble only. "It was … it was pretty frightening."

"Can you tell us what happened?" Scott asked.

"Um, well, it went pretty fast," Samuel said, licking his lips. I wondered how nervous he was, on a scale of one to ten. I would have conservatively estimated he was a twenty-eight.

"What do you remember?" I asked. I'd like to say I did it soothingly, but he flinched as I spoke, so I probably sailed wide of the mark on that one.

"Umm, not much."

"Do you remember the perp's face?" Scott leaned on the counter, and by the way he asked, I could tell he was playing good cop. His voice was gentle, friendly, like he was your buddy about to take you out for a beer after work.

"Not really," Samuel said, and he shifted his eyes nervously toward me. He wasn't lying, I didn't think. Poor guy was probably traumatized. I sighed loudly, and he looked like he wanted to take a step back from the counter.

I held out my hand for him to shake. "Thanks for your cooperation."

Scott gave me a puzzled, sidelong look, probably wondering why I was ready to give up the interrogation so soon. I didn't dignify his look by returning it, just kept staring straight ahead at Samuel and tried to make myself smile without looking like I was going to lean over the counter and drink his blood. It wasn't easy.

"Uh, okay." Samuel took my hand, giving it a gentle shake. "Anything I can do to help." He started to pull away, but I held firm. "Umm."

"Just a second." I leaned forward, keeping his hand trapped in mine. If Charlie had been here, she would have cooed at him, done something seductive to keep his attention off the fact that I had his hand in an iron grip.

I'm not Charlie.

"I … uh …" Samuel looked like he wanted to sputter and started to tug his hand away from me again. It had been about seven seconds, and things were far beyond awkward. "I … I need my hand back."

"I said wait." My voice was steel, and the command caused Samuel to freeze. His eyes went wide, his freckled face fell, and for a moment I thought he'd die of sheer terror right then.

A second later, the pain started at a low burn, and I could tell by the look on his face that it took everything he had not to start screaming.

Chapter 13

It was a funny feeling, touching someone's soul the way I could. It always started with the burning; my flesh pressed against theirs in a nearly intimate way. I stared into Annoying Samuel's eyes, and saw green irises peeking back at me between eyelids tightened in fear.

I didn't care if he screamed, not now. I could feel his mind, there for the taking, and I leapt right in. I'd rifled through a few heads in my time, using my soul-draining powers to go through memories the way a clerk could pull files out of a filing cabinet.

This one was easy to find. Everyone's head was a little different, at least the ones I'd been in. Samuel's was organized to the point of being annoying, like he had preplanned so he could live up to my expectations of him.

I shouldn't complain; it actually made my job easier. As I slid into his memory, the world around me faded. Whenever I stole a memory, I could view it as though it were taking place around me, while my surroundings slowed and disappeared. The pawnshop around me became a dull wash of blue tones, like the world had been filtered through a navy crystal.

The door opened behind me as I heard a ding-dong electronic tone that I hadn't even noticed as I had entered the pawnshop. I stood in front of the counter and turned to see Samuel behind me, working on a clipboard on top of the glass countertop. The place was nearly empty.

Samuel looked up as the patron entered. The face was blurred, and I had to concentrate on it. I pushed through the blurring like brushing aside snow on a windshield. It took me a minute but it faded and I could see a face. I had looked through a lot of memories, but I couldn't recall ever seeing anything like the blurring effect before.

"Can I help you?" Samuel asked. He was leaning on the counter with both elbows, and his tone was polite but harried. Clearly in the middle of something important. Or something self-important, more likely. Like keeping a flawless inventory.

I looked at the guy entering. Once I got past the blur, I could tell—barely—through the blue tinge of the world that he was darker of skin, Latino maybe. His face looked slightly pinched, like he was walking with a pebble in his shoe. Or a boulder.

"Empty the cash register," the guy said as he walked over to the counter. He wasn't shuffling exactly, but he was at a hurried pace that didn't quite match with his facial expression. Was he limping? The memory was so fuzzy. Bizarre.

"Excuse me?" Samuel's tone was still polite, like he hadn't heard what the guy said.

The guy took two more quick strides to the counter and had Samuel by the throat before the clerk could even flinch away. "I'm sorry," the guy said, and he was truly apologetic. "I need the money in your cash register. Now." There was an urgency there, driven by some deep emotion. I suspected fear.

The door dinged behind him, and the new guy turned. Another stranger was standing in the doorway, this one a little broader of shoulder. Big guy, probably over six feet tall. He wore dark sunglasses and a trench coat, which I thought was beyond weird for Vegas in the dead of summer. There was another shadowed figure just a pace behind him, a woman by the looks of her. She was shorter, stocky, and that was all I could see of her. She was hidden in a cloud of blur so deep that even when I focused on her, she still looked like she was standing behind smoky glass.

"Get out of here," the robber told them. Now his fear was obvious, even to Samuel, who he still held by the neck. I looked around the shop and marveled at how a normally crisp memory was completely degraded to the point where I was having trouble making out anything. I stared at Samuel, wondering if he perhaps had glasses that he'd forgotten to wear. A quick check of his outside mind showed that no, in fact, his other memories were clear as HD video. No blue, no blur.

Trenchcoat did not answer. I stared at him and saw the blurring fade enough to make out his face. It was a broad face, a flat one, like he'd been hit in the nose with a frying pan every day of his life. He took another step into the shop and paused. He wore a smile, and from the look of it I got more than a hint of malevolence. He had some serious ill intentions for the robber, and things started to click into place for me.

"Get out!" The robber shouted, voice cracking with the strain.

"Antonio Morales," Trenchcoat said, his dark eyes and face made even more sinister by that damned blurring effect, "this is the end." I wanted to reach out and slap the bastard for saying anything as ominous and cheesy as he had, but I wasn't exactly corporeal in this memory.

Morales was shaking, his hand still wrapped around Samuel's neck. He carried the look of a doomed man on his face, fighting to keep the horror submerged and failing. I could empathize.

"Just leave me alone," Morales said, nearly pleading. "Just go."

Trenchcoat took another step in, then another. I could tell by the look on his face that he was savoring it. This bastard loved the fear he was causing. He lived for this. It was all right there on his face—he was going to hurt Antonio, was going to kill him. And he'd enjoy every minute of it.

I could see the cascade of emotions on Antonio Morales's face, and then they just stopped. His mouth turned to a thin line, his grip on Samuel's neck slackened and he let the clerk go. Samuel fell back as Morales's hand went to his waist, and I barely saw him pull the gun before it was out and firing.

Antonio Morales filled the air with bullets. I saw one of them catch Trenchcoat perfectly in the forehead, and a puff of red spit out the back of his skull and painted the glass windows. Trenchcoat's look was utter surprise, then he pitched forward and landed with all the grace of a felled tree. And most of the noise, too.

Samuel let out a scream that tore through the shop. Antonio kept his piece pointed at the door, and I could see that the woman, the one who had been so heavily blurred, was gone. Smart move. Even a meta could be killed by a gun, as Trenchcoat had just proven.

And he was dead. I took a moment to drop to the ground to check. His lips were hanging open, saliva streaming out. I was surprised there was no blood, like you see in movies. I mean, there was some pooling on the ground beneath him, but none dribbling out of his mouth. He was still, and his breath had already left him. He didn't look familiar at all, but that didn't matter.

I knew who he was. Or at least, who he was with, and that was close enough.

Antonio was shaking, standing in the same spot where he'd started the robbery. I thought for a minute he was going to collapse on the countertop and lose it right there, but he pulled himself together and shoved the gun into the front of his waistband, the hammer still cocked. I cringed when I noticed he didn't safety it first. Bad idea, Antonio. All it'd take was the slightest pressure on the trigger next time he pulled it and suddenly Antonio would become Antonia.

Antonio gave a quick look around the store. Annoying Samuel was still against the wall, shaking but now upright. I could feel it when Antonio had grabbed him, and the hold was strong, like a meta's. Still, he wouldn't have known that, and it made me wonder what could possibly have clued our people in that this was a meta incident.

"I'm sorry," Antonio said, and the remorse was all over his face.

His eyes were sagging, his lips were drawn down like he'd had someone pull his cheeks down with lead weights. I thought he was going to cry right there for just a beat. He turned to Trenchcoat, and for just a moment I thought he was going to apologize to the corpse, too. The smell of gunfire hung heavy in the air.

"Uh …" Samuel's answer was a non-answer, two steps away from stuttering. His mouth hung open and he tried to form words. He lifted a hand to point, and it shook like he was in agonizing pain at that very moment. "I … I'm afraid I'm going to have to ask you to leave …" I just stared at him, glad I was incorporeal. I doubt I could have hid how much I was marveling at his stupidity.

"I'll go," Antonio said, to my surprise. He shook for a moment, and his skin rippled. He grunted like it hurt, his skin taking on a different texture, a rougher one. He grunted again, and I wondered if he was going to Hulk out like a Hercules-type. His body stayed the same shape, though, his skin just … changed. And not like I'd seen Clyde Clary do.

Ridges appeared as his body hardened and he gained a few inches in height. Antonio started toward the door and his walk was even slower and more awkward than before, like he was walking on two tree trunks. Like one of the Ents I'd seen in the Lord of the Rings movies. His hips swung wide with every step and he went through the door sideways, shuffling to accommodate his larger frame. His skin had become like tree bark, a layer of protection against whatever came his way.

I watched him walk, and changed my angle slightly to see him go for a car across the street. He lurched toward it, and as he reached the side I caught a glimpse of the plate number.

I took one last look at Samuel, against the wall, watching, hand still shaking and stuck in place from where he'd held it out to point Antonio toward the door.

The memory faded as the pawnshop snapped back into rough clarity around me. The haze of blue was gone, and I realized that the blurring had faded as soon as the stocky woman had run away from the scene. I pulled my hand from Samuel's and his body slackened, slumping onto the counter. He caught himself with a hand, but he looked as though he was going to be sick right there on the glass display. Which would be a shame, because then the next customer wouldn't be able to see the ten thousand Pokemon games he had for sale.

"Wha …" Samuel's green eyes snapped up to me, cloudy, like he was coming out of a deep sleep. "What … what …" He murmured, nearly incoherent.

"Go sit down," I said, turning away. I started back toward the door, the neon signs that lit the front windows looking even more vivid now that I'd returned from the haze of memory. "You've had a very traumatic experience."

"I … have?" Samuel mumbled. "Did I get robbed again?"

I paused, thinking of all the things I'd like to say, the things that would sound cool, but the truth was, he was a scared kid. I'd seen that while I was in his mind. He wasn't any older than me, and he was so bad with people he'd probably be single forever. "No," I said. "You're going to be fine. You just got a little lightheaded there for a bit. Have a seat, chill out and get some water, okay?"

"Okay," he said as I pushed through the door into the sweltering Vegas heat.

The bright sun overhead glared down on me. This time I started to sweat instantly, but it still felt like my body was retaining heat so it could cook me internally. I made it five steps before Scott opened up on me. I'd almost forgotten he was there, he'd gotten so quiet.

"What the hell was that?" He didn't even bother to restrain his anger; it lashed at me as we walked through the sweltering parking lot.

"Investigation," I said.

"You almost took that poor bastard's soul!"

"I was at least ten seconds away from that," I replied, heading for the car. This time, I felt a trickle of sweat make its way from under my hair down my temple. "Besides, I got a plate number for the robber and some insight into what's going on."

Scott paused, and I could feel his anger without looking at him. He was a black hole of irritation, following just behind me. "What did you find out?" he asked finally, with reluctance, like he was being dragged to the point of asking.

"Antonio—the robber—got interrupted by Century," I said. "He pulled a gun and shot one of their members." I glanced back at the store. "Killed him. And it saved Antonio's life."

"Great," Scott said, and let loose a sigh. "So the extermination is alive and well in Vegas right now. Or was, anyway."

"Still is, I think." I reached the car and grasped for the handle. The chrome was so hot from the sun that it burned my hand. "There was another one of them—a telepath. She blurred the world for Samuel so he couldn't remember much of anything."

Scott let that sink in. "Why … why would she care?"

I'd been thinking about that since I'd figured out what she was doing, and I'd come to a conclusion that made me smile. "Because if the extermination is going on right now, here in Vegas, then it means the last of Century's telepaths are here. Right now." I glanced at Scott and saw him nod, all trace of his rage gone.

In fact, I think he might have smiled just a little bit himself.

Chapter 14

The Las Vegas Metropolitan PD got us a near-instantaneous return on Antonio Morales's license plate, along with an address that was in Henderson. Fortunately, I found out when I checked the GPS that we were in fact already in Henderson, and our destination was less than ten minutes away.

"I guess Antonio doesn't adhere to the old adage of 'Don't shit where you live,'" Scott said. He chuckled slightly.

I frowned, feeling a surprising amount of empathy for the would-be stick-up artist. "He was scared. He knew Century was coming after him, somehow."

"If that's the case, you don't think he's going to be hanging around his house, do you?" Scott sent me a sidelong look that I ignored.

We pulled up to the house a few minutes later. It looked odd to me after a steady couple years of Minnesota living. The entire front yard was made up of rocks instead of grass, and instead of the paneling that was so common in the upper Midwest, the exterior was a dull beige stucco texture that reminded me of a choppy river. The whole neighborhood had a similar sun-bleached look, complete with dull orange roofing tiles that reminded me of an Italian villa I'd seen on TV.

"We're not in Minneapolis anymore," Scott said, neck hunched down to look at the house.

"What tipped you off?" I jerked the handle of the car and pushed the door open. "The hundred and eight degree temperature?" I felt the rush of heat hit me again as I stepped out onto the sidewalk.

"Well, really, it was that there's no lawn," Scott said,

straightening as he got out of the car. "What's up with that?"

"It's the desert," I said with a shrug.

"Yeah, but I've seen grass. They've got golf courses here. It's not all sand, sand, sand as far as the eye can see. I mean, Las Vegas means 'the meadows' in Spanish, for crying out loud."

"Do I look like a climatologist or something?" I asked, but said it relatively gently. My nerves were getting to me. I had no idea what to do here, and standing out in the hot sun wasn't making me any happier or more relaxed. I wondered how long it would take my pale ass to get sunburned. I looked at my lily-white, near-glowing skin and knew that it wouldn't take long. Not in this heat.

We walked up the driveway, past the single brown garage door. I opened the metal gate attached to the front door and gave it a solid knock. The whole setup screamed, "Go away!" to me, and I wondered if it was a function of the owner's personality or just the neighborhood that prompted it. The streets were quiet, filled with houses just like this, but it was hard to tell if it was quiet because people were scared, or if it was just too hot to be out.

I felt a long trickle of sweat roll down my ribs and started leaning toward the latter.

I gave the door another solid knock. Scott and I waited, staring at each other for a good thirty seconds before he broke the silence. "Maybe he's not home," he said.

"Maybe." I gave it a second's thought and then kicked down the door.

"Jesus, Sienna!" Scott said, and he had his gun drawn a second later. I was already on my way inside. "Are you trying to get killed?"

"Antonio," I announced from the entryway. "My name is Sienna Nealon and I'm here to talk to you."

There was a stark silence. "I don't think I'd believe you if I were him," Scott said. "You just kicked down his door!"

"I don't think he's here," I said, chewing my lip. It was dry and starting to crack from the desert air. "I suspect Century ran him to ground."

"You mean like … he's dead?" Scott asked.

"Or hiding." I couldn't see anything from the entryway, so I took a step forward and looked to my right. Just through an arch was a living room that had been tossed. And by tossed I mean completely destroyed in the search for anything useful. The couches were knocked over, the cushions slashed to leave a mess of stuffing everywhere on the grey slate tile. The coffee table was overturned, presumably when someone checked to make sure nothing was taped underneath. There were holes punched in the walls, vases shattered, and every painting had been torn down and ripped from its frame.

"Ugly, but thorough," Scott said, going down the hall. He still had his gun out and peeked around the corner with his weapon first. "Kitchen."

I followed him past the kitchen and into bedrooms, my pistol drawn now as well. I didn't think we'd find either Century or Morales, but I'd been trained that it was better to be safe than sorry. We swept through the house, clearing it before we searched in depth for clues to the whereabouts of Antonio Morales.

Once we were sure no one was there, we ended up in a bedroom that looked to have been re-purposed as an office and a garden. There were dozens of potted plants, and every pot had been smashed. Clay fragments littered the wood floor like broken pieces of Antonio Morales's life. There was a computer here, too, and it looked like it was the only thing that hadn't been smashed and overturned. Scott gave it a nod then touched the mouse to wake it. "What's up with this?"

"Probably searched his computer as best they could," I said as the screen turned right back into a desert landscape. "Looked under the table rather than turning it over, and just left it when they were done."

"Huh." Scott leaned over and opened the browser. "History's clear. I guess Antonio covered his tracks pretty well."

"Yeah," I said and gently put a hand on him. He looked up in surprise and I pushed him aside. Not hard, more like a suggestion to move. With a minor amount of force. I reached down and typed an IP address into the bar at the top of the browser and hit enter. I saw it load then enter a blank screen as I pulled out my phone and dialed a contact.

"Hello, Boss Lady," came J.J.'s high voice from the other end of the line. He sounded awfully peppy.

"I just pinged your site from a computer I need searched," I said.

"Ahhh, I just got an alert about that," J.J. said. "Henderson, Nevada, huh? Put a dollar in the slot machine for me, will ya?"

"I'll get right on that," I muttered. "Give me something, J.J."

"Hmmmm," he said. "Looks like somebody worked this computer over. Twelve days ago a buttload of files were erased, browser history cleared. Six days ago someone nosed around looking for stuff, copied the remains of the hard drive to a flash drive. Doesn't look like they found anything."

"And will you find anything?" I asked.

There was a laugh on the other end of the line that bordered on boastful. "I already have, because I'm not some amateur loser that gets halted in his tracks by a blanked-out browser history. I am—"

"*I* am not renowned for my patience," I said, cutting him off, "so let that be your guide in whatever you say next."

There was a moment's silence from the phone. "Right. Yes. Okay. So, I have his search history, thanks to some back doors we have with the big providers—"

"English is my primary language, and it would help me greatly if you'd speak it to me," I said.

There was another pause. "Okay, well, short answer—I don't have anything for you right now."

"Remember what I said earlier about patience?"

"But I can get you some analysis!" J.J. said. "I just need some time. I've got his search history, I've got some files he failed to erase properly, I mean there's a lot of stuff for me to work with. Give me a few hours to sort it out, okay? Please?" Now he sounded like he was begging.

I held my breath for effect, and I imagined I could hear him doing the same on the other end of the line, but for entirely different reasons. "Fine," I said. "Hurry." And I hung up.

"You were kind of harsh with J.J.," Scott observed as we made our way down the darkened hallway toward the front door. "I don't think I've ever heard you manage anyone else like that."

"J.J. is special," I said, thinking of something pretty gross that I'd inferred from something he'd told me about his cat. Scott was right, though; I didn't usually lean on people—at least not my allies—the way I'd just leaned on him. Maybe the stress was getting to me.

"Uh huh." I could hear the reticence in the way he said it.

My phone began to ring. "See?" I said, but I didn't smile. Dammit, he'd actually made me feel bad about how I'd treated J.J. I looked at the faceplate but didn't immediately recognize the number. It had a 702 area code, which I knew meant it was local. I slid my finger across the answer button. "Hello?"

"Hi, is this Sienna?" There was a kind of nervous tentativeness in the voice. "It's Lauren over at the morgue."

"Oh, hey," I said as I got into the car. Scott fired it up and the air conditioner started blowing at full blast, warm air that hadn't had a chance to cool just yet. "What's up?"

There was a pause. "Huh. Kind of weird to hear an FBI agent ask 'what's up?'"

I felt my face crease in a frown. "I'm young yet. What can I do for you?"

"I was calling about your aunt's autopsy report. We got back something … interesting."

"Oh?" I reined in my desire to tell her to get on with it, too, and just waited.

"Yeah, about that wound on her abdomen." I could hear the shuffle of papers in the background. "It was really weird."

I waited to see if she was going to make me guess. "Tell me more," I said, not entirely without sarcasm.

"Well, it's not a knife wound," she said. "Not a blade at all. In fact …" She paused, and I could hear her taking a breath, marshaling herself as though she were about to deliver bad news, "… it looks like it was delivered by a fingernail, or something similar, like—"

"Like a claw," I said and felt a chill even though the car was still blowing nothing but hot air.

Chapter 15

"So who do you think it is?" Scott asked after we'd parked in the Palazzo's garage and walked inside. He hadn't said anything on the ride back to the hotel, giving me time to collect my thoughts.

I felt my skin readjust to the cool air inside the Palazzo and pushed my lips around. It took me a second to realize I was probably making a duck face, so I stopped. "I don't know. Lots of metas have claws, or something like them. Wolfe did, Bastet did."

"Mmhmm," Scott said, almost unconsciously. We walked down the hall, and I admired the white granite-looking tile. Wait, was that actually granite? These casinos went all-out. "What about this Antonio Morales guy?" Scott asked. "What kind of powers did he have? Tree skin?"

"Something like that," I said. I hadn't really seen anything quite like it, other than Clary. "Walked like a tree, developed skin like a tree—you ever heard of anything like that?"

"Dryad, maybe?" Scott said with a shrug. "Sounds like something I read about once."

"Dryad." I tried to remember where I'd read about them. The Directorate had always been pretty cagey about their knowledge of specific meta types, something I'd always thought odd until Old Man Winter betrayed me. I had wondered more than a few times since if his goal had been to keep us in the dark so we wouldn't assume someone was a certain type and get blindsided by a surprise power, or if he had more sinister reasons for keeping types a secret. "Like a wood nymph?"

"Sort of," Scott said, and his face was all frown. We passed by a restaurant and the smell of lovely fried things caught me in its thrall. I wanted to eat, right now, and make it ALL THE FOOD.

My stomach tugged me in one direction, my feet kept me moving toward the elevator bank, through the casino floor. "You hungry?"

"Unbelievably," I said. "But I should probably check in with Ariadne and see if we can get some info on this dryad or whatever, and maybe see if we can wrangle up a possible explanation for this claw mystery. If we could even narrow it down a little, it might give us something to go on—"

"Yeah, it'll be a great list of metas with long fingernails," Scott said with a weary sigh. "This being Vegas, maybe it was Howard Hughes." The sound of the slot machines jingled and jangled all around us. "I'm starving."

I realized for the first time he looked more than a little disheveled. His eyes were drawn and tired, and his usual color was off by a couple degrees. He'd been up since long before the break of day trying to hunt down leads for me, and he'd endured last night in worried silence thanks to me. "Why don't you go get something to eat? I'll go back to the room and try to get these things nailed down. It'll probably only take a few minutes, and I'll come back to join you." I was also feeling really sweaty and wanted to change clothes and shower, but that wasn't information he needed.

"Yeah, all right," he said, and I could feel his reluctance. Whether it was because he didn't want to part from me or because he didn't want to eat lunch alone, I didn't push. "I'll … just go in here." He pointed to the café we'd just passed, eight rows of slot machines back. "Come on down when you're done. I might, uh … play for a few minutes first while I wait for you."

"Don't wait on my account; I could be a while." I tried to smile sweetly, but I suspected my face didn't allow for that. It probably came off as a cringe. "But if you do end up playing, put in a dollar for J.J., will you?"

He gave me a nod and turned around as I headed off without him. The elevators were ahead, past a rolling wheel of rainbow-colored lights. It spun around and around, a number up in the millions lit next to it. I thought about that amount of money for a moment and then promptly dismissed it. I was pretty well paid at this point, as I had always been. Even if I had all that money, it wouldn't solve the problems I had. The genocide of my people and my impending status as Sovereign's sweetheart weren't going to be solved no matter how many zeroes I added to my bank account.

I stepped into the little alcove containing the elevator bank and stood there after pressing the button. My stomach was bothering me now, irritated that I'd fed it nothing but grease so far today. It rumbled at me, and I turned to look longingly at the casino floor, where, somewhere down the line, the restaurant waited.

I pressed a sweaty palm against my jeans and wiped them against the denim. I bitched about the cold when it was winter in Minnesota, but this heat was just too much for me. I could feel the sticky film of dried sweat all over my body. I shifted my stance, staring onto the casino floor as I waited for the ding to herald the elevator's arrival. This morning's stale coffee still dominated my taste buds. It was funny how I hated the stuff, but I still drank it by the gallon since I had taken my new role.

My eyes alighted on a woman just outside the elevator alcove as I heard the dinging sound I'd been waiting for. She was stocky, with longer hair, and features that were in sharp clarity. She was watching me, it took me only a second to realize, and once I realized it, she snapped into a blurry field in the middle of my vision, like someone had nearly erased her from my sight.

I felt my muscles tighten and my hands clench. I thundered out of the elevator alcove to find her already gone, whether because of the mind game she'd just played on me or because she'd moved, I wasn't sure.

I looked down the casino floor as I ran. Slot machines spun and whirled in a musical chorus. My feet pounded against the granite floors and I dodged tourists left and right as I ran at full speed back toward the café.

I threw up a hope that I wouldn't be too late as I rounded the last corner and barely avoided colliding with a waitress carrying a tray of drinks. She cursed at me and I leapt over her. Cries of surprise and awe came from behind me and I ignored every one of them.

I caught sight of Scott as I reached the apex of my jump. He stood on the tile walkway that ran through the middle of the casino, at the center of a triangle made up of three men in suits. Three burly men. Like Trenchcoat.

Surrounded.

Chapter 16

I was only about twenty feet away from him when the pain racked through my skull like someone had split it open with a fire axe. I dropped to my knees like I'd lost all muscle control. My momentum carried me into a roll and I crashed into a slot machine.

Metas run fast. I'd been clocked once by Dr. Sessions at slightly north of thirty miles per hour on a sprint. I wasn't going quite that fast when the telepath shut down my legs for a second, but I had to be going at least fifteen or twenty miles an hour. In a car accident, even with seatbelts and a metal chassis to protect you, a twenty-mile per hour collision is still nothing to sneeze at.

For an unprotected body, slamming into the ground so hard you roll into a metal and glass machine? Ouch.

I hit the base of the slot machine so hard I felt it rock. Glass shattered and showered down on me. There were spots in my vision that couldn't be accounted for by the flashing lights of the casino. The world seemed to be moving, and I wondered if the machine was teetering.

Then it fell on me.

I thought about the time Wolfe had grabbed me by the throat and tried to throttle the life out of me. I thought about a fight I'd had with Bjorn that felt like the world was ending around me. About the time I'd gotten punched by a guy named Henderschott who was wearing a metal suit.

I'm not sure any of them were worse than the slot machine landing on me.

My arm went immediately numb from mid-humerus down to my fingers. Like it had been cut off. I wondered if it had been severed, and if there should have been phantom pain. All the pain I was feeling elsewhere was as decidedly un-phantom as you could get. My ribs screamed at me like someone had split them open with a maul down my right side. Blood filled my mouth.

I fought for a breath, and every second of it hurt. I gasped and the bloody spittle shot out of my mouth, flecking my face. There were voices around me, but the pain was so great I couldn't pay any attention to them. I could feel my left hand and arm, jutting out from beneath my body. The rest of me was pinned.

Sounds of panic, of angry shouts, reached my ears over the dinging of another slot machine. The sound of coins pouring out of somewhere was like a staccato rain—unending in its intensity. Funny, it didn't feel like I'd won the jackpot for anything but agony.

I tried to move my trapped arm again, to no avail. Bright lights shone down above. White, constant lights, a contrast to the multicolored, flashing ones that surrounded me from the gambling machines.

The pain.

Ohhhhh, the pain.

"Sienna," came a voice from above me. I tilted my head to look up. There was a face standing between me and the bright, white light above. "Don't worry. We won't hurt you."

I would have replied, something snappy, something witty, but I couldn't get enough breath to do it. Or enough wit to come up with something worthy. Instead I grunted.

"What's that?" There was far too much amusement in that voice for my taste. I saw her face; it was that damned stocky telepath. She wasn't even bothering to blur it anymore; she knew she had me. If I hadn't been trapped and in agony, I would have—

"Oh, but you are trapped," she said, almost cooing. "I think we'll just leave you there after we finish with your friend."

Damned telepaths. Always one step ahead. Except …

She'd stepped closer to me for comic effect, wearing a satin sundress that probably did more to help her manage the heat than anything I had in my wardrobe.

But it also left her calf exposed.

I clamped my left hand around her ankle and ripped it from underneath her. She went down, hard and awkward. Hell, if I hadn't been trapped underneath a slot machine fighting for every breath, I would have been laughing at her. Because misery, that's why.

I couldn't see her hit the ground, but I heard and felt it. She made a satisfying smack as she landed. I twisted her ankle until I heard it break, until I heard her scream. Then I twisted it further. I felt the resistance as her knee reached its limit, and then I pushed past it.

I felt the tendons and flesh rip as I put a hold on her dancing career. Then I shoved, hard, pushing her tibia out through the hole I'd made in her skin by the kneecap. I was pretty sure she was in the most agonizing pain I'd ever put anyone in.

Oddly enough, I was totally okay with that.

The taunting telepath dealt with, I turned back to the slot machine crushing the life out of me. I was one of the strongest people on the planet, dammit. I wasn't about to be trapped under a reverse ATM machine while Scott was blindsided by Century. No matter how heavy it was.

I gave it a hard push. The numbness I had felt in the middle of my bicep turned to pain in one hell of a hurry but I gritted it back. Hadn't I beaten my way through a metal door a year ago? With my bare hands?

I pushed again, grunting. I expelled all the air in my body and felt the machine rock slightly.

I needed leverage. It rolled back onto me, making my ribs cry out again. I rolled back, trying to get enough momentum to turn it onto its side. It tilted, and I forced it up harder.

I felt the weight of the slot machine leave me, and it was the greatest feeling ever. It was like someone had pulled a bulldozer off my body after leaving it parked there during a weekend bender. They'd run me over a few times before they managed to get the damned thing gone.

After it was off, I lay there for what felt like a year, but was probably less than thirty seconds. I rolled to my knees and started working my way up, very slowly. My legs seemed to be unharmed, probably because my arm and chest had taken the brunt of the machine's impact.

I looked up and Scott was there, in the middle of the three Century metas. He had one by the face, palm cupped around his nose and mouth, and I could see water spraying from the meta's eyes and from behind Scott's iron grip on his face. After a few seconds he stopped resisting, and Scott let the body drop to the ground. I watched bloody water seep across the granite floor.

I glanced back to make sure the telepath was still down. Her right leg looked like she had no shin, like all the skin of her lower leg had been clumped up. Her foot was sticking out of that knob of flesh, just below her knee, and bones were jutting at forty-five degree angles out of her knee joint.

"And stay down," I told her, but I doubt she heard me over her own muffled crying. She was rolling around a lot. I didn't feel bad for her, though, for some reason. Possibly because I still couldn't feel my right arm.

I tested the arm as I headed toward Scott. I couldn't feel it, but it moved. If it was broken, it didn't seem like it, and that's all I needed. I let it hang and tilted it in a circle at the shoulder. No problems. I tried to bend it at the elbow and that didn't go so well. It was like a case of dead arm. Slow, unwieldy. Not useless in a fight, but near to it.

Part of me wanted to throw a slot machine at the two guys who were left. Now that I wasn't trapped beneath one with a useless arm, I suspected I could have lifted one easily enough. Wouldn't that have been ironic? Unfortunately, that was probably one of those things that would require both hands.

Scott was keeping both of the guys at bay with a spray of water. I knew how hard he could hit with those things, and I suspected he could keep them occupied for a while longer. He blasted one of them full on and the guy staggered back, crashing into a roulette table and flipping onto the top of it. The croupier and customers had long since fled, and I could see a perimeter of gawkers standing at a safe distance, watching the biggest fight Las Vegas had seen since the last time Floyd Mayweather had been in town.

I didn't have time to wonder what they were thinking of a man spraying water from his hands, though. It was the town that made Siegfried and Roy famous, after all; hopefully they thought it was just an impromptu stage-less show.

I picked the nearest Century target and came at him low. I hit him in a tackle with my shoulder. I could feel and hear his vertebra snap in his lower back. I clamped a hand on his neck and yanked it back for good measure. The bones broke there, too, once I applied enough pressure to them, and the man went limp in my grasp.

Once upon a time, killing had been hard for me. Now, injured and in a fight where Scott's life could be in jeopardy, it wasn't even a question. I could not let this guy get back up, because the results of my failure to stop him now could mean someone else's death.

And I realized, as I listened to his spine pop when I forced his neck down, that I was long past the point where I was willing to accept the deaths of my friends because of my failure to act responsibly. Leaving my enemies alive—Weissman, Sovereign, Winter—had caused me and mine more pain than I cared to think about. Breandan had died because Weissman had ordered a raid on the Agency campus. Others had died with him. Because I had left Weissman alive when I shouldn't have.

I killed that nameless Century thug and realized—not for the first time and not without extreme discomfort—that maybe Old Man Winter had been right all along.

I dropped the body to the ground with a thump. Scott's eyes met mine and we both turned to the last guy. He was watching us from the roulette table, dark eyes buried under a scar that ran the length of his forehead and carried a jagged edge to it. He pulled himself off the table as we watched, then glanced back and readjusted a pile of chips on the table. "Forty-two red," he said under his breath.

"Putting all your money on one number doesn't seem all that bright," Scott said. I cocked my eye and looked at him. It didn't feel like the moment for a discussion of the long odds involved in gambling.

"Sometimes you need to bet big on the long shot," the scarred guy said with a smile. He had a lot more self-assurance than I would have given a lowly flunky credit for. His goatee and hair were all deep black, flecked with just a little grey. He was a meta who looked like he was in his forties, so I guessed he was probably at least a thousand.

And he was one of the hundred Century picked to wage its war.

"What's your name?" I asked, clutching my still-numb arm to my side. I flexed my right hand, and could feel a hint of feeling restored to it.

"Do you care?" There was a glint of amusement in his eyes. They were lively, like he was in on a joke that none of the rest of us would get.

"Only a little," I said. "You know you're not walking out of here alive, don't you?"

His smile was wider than mine would have been in his place. "I sense that's what you believe."

"You believe differently?" I didn't look away from him.

His grin was infectious, yet somehow I didn't match it.

Anywhere else, I might have liked this guy. He was self-aware, and I sensed more charm than he wanted to let on. "It doesn't matter what I believe." His voice was low, and I detected the hint of an accent, far underneath it all. "I can't hurt you."

"Oh, yeah?" I held up my right arm a little limply. "Sadly, your friend the telepath did not feel the same."

"You'll be fine," he said, and I caught a hint of mournfulness. "You're a stone killer now, after all."

"Do you know me?" I asked. I could see security guards coming to our left and right, following the white granite tile path right to us. Scott flipped out his FBI badge and held it up. I watched them all stop. Watching. Waiting.

"I know you," he said. His dark eyes were on me. "And I don't envy you. Because I know what lies in front of you, and it scared me bad enough to join them rather than go against what they wanted." He had looked so large when he'd been facing off with Scott. Now he looked small, and a lifetime of infinite regret was etched on his face. He was older than a thousand.

"What's your name?" I asked him again, gently this time. That surprised even me. The security guards watching us had guns drawn, but they were still holding their distance. I could hear Scott urging them to stay back, but almost all my attention was on my adversary.

"You know my name," he said, and that infectious grin was back. "Everyone knows my name now. Movies, pop culture. They all know the trickster, the mischief-maker." He took a step toward me. "You killed my last surviving brother, you know." His smile disappeared. "So you know me. And I know you, Sienna Nealon."

He reached in his coat, and somehow I knew what he was going to do before he did it. There was a gun in his hand when it came back out, and I felt the chill as a memory breathed over me, a voice from somewhere in the back of my head.

It's not real.

The shot rang out from behind me, and the smiling man who wouldn't tell me his name had a third eye blasted into the middle of his forehead. I glanced back and saw Scott with his pistol out. It was the finest shot I'd ever seen him make.

The man fell to his knees, already dead, a line of blood running down his nose. He slumped sideways and landed on his arm. There was no gun. His hands were empty, his expression vacant, and I knew this was what he wanted. Of all the choices he could have made, this was the one that was most palatable to him.

"Are you all right?" Scott was at my shoulder. His breath was stale and rank. "Did he—"

"I'm fine," I said, and glanced at the body of a man who'd lived for thousands of years. "He tricked you. Got you to do his dirty work for him." Part of me wanted to smile. After all, this was one less enemy on the playing field.

There was another part of me that felt considerably more torn. This was one less meta left on the planet. Because of Sovereign. Because of Weissman. Because of Century.

"I don't think he was ever as bad as everyone thought he was," I muttered, more to myself than anything.

"What?" Scott asked, and I could see his brow crumple. "That guy just tried to kill me."

"Yeah," I said. "But still. He was so scared of Sovereign and Weissman that he would have rather died than face them."

"Sucks to be him?" Scott's eyes were wide in near-alarm. "Are you seriously taking his side on this one? The dude made his choice. He was a villain through and through." He frowned and looked at the body. "Where did the gun go?"

I glanced back at the corpse. Casino security was poking at him, probably looking for the weapon, but it was pointless. "Don't you get it? There was no gun. It was an illusion."

I took the slow walk away, around the next row of slot machines. Security kept an eye on me the whole time, but I didn't care. I couldn't leave the scene because I needed to talk to the cops. Give a statement. Spout some bullshit that would preserve our identities and cover up what happened here. I had an idea about that.

I took one last look back at the body laid out in front of the roulette wheel. I heard a voice, deep in my mind, from Bjorn, and I let him speak through me. For me. Because he couldn't.

"Goodbye, Loki."

Chapter 17

"What are you still doing in Vegas?" Senator Foreman's voice was stern and tight, laced with disapproval through and through.

"High jinks, mostly." I was sitting in my suite in the Palazzo, in bed. Management had comped us the cost of the place for the night. I'd done some delicate manipulation of Century's telepath by twirling her exposed bones around, and she'd helpfully kept the swarms of LVMPD that came to investigate from remembering to check the security feed. In return, I'd stopped twisting her tibia. It was not exactly my finest hour, but when you're tasked with keeping a secret, sometimes you have to use whatever means you have at your disposal. "Actually, always high jinks." I felt a frown coming on. "How'd you even know I was here?"

"Las Vegas PD called the Minneapolis FBI field office to verify your credentials," Foreman's terse reply came from the other end of the line. "Because apparently you trashed a casino."

"That is an exaggeration." I twirled my index finger along the edge of the sheet, felt the satin against my skin. It was nice and cool in here, thankfully. "It was one slot machine. And maybe some water damage to a roulette table." I paused to think about it. "Bloodstains aren't permanent, are they?"

"You would know better than I would." When Foreman spoke again, it was with even more tension. "What are you doing? Aren't you supposed to be protecting your people in Minneapolis?"

"I fell into the middle of the extinction here," I said. "Some of Century's goons made a run at us, so we took care of it. If they've really only got a hundred people, we've successfully lowered that number to about ninety now."

"Forgive me for not being ecstatic that you've solved ten

percent of our problem," Foreman said, employing more than a little sarcasm himself. I wondered if he ever spoke like that on the Senate floor. C-Span would be much more exciting if he did.

"You're forgiven," I said breezily. "Anyway, I've got one last loose end to tie up here, then I'll be on a plane back to Minneapolis."

There was a long pause. "What's really going on, Sienna?" All sarcasm had been laid aside.

"I'm just …" I looked up. Scott was still in the bathroom, and I could hear the shower running. "You've put me in charge of an awful lot, Senator. I'm doing the best I can. We've had some … setbacks, that's all."

"You mean how you met Sovereign and couldn't lay a hand on him?"

I tasted something sharp and acidic in my mouth, and it wasn't the blood that I was still getting tastes of every now and again. "I'll be the first to admit that didn't help."

"I recruited you to this job because you were the only person I had run across that was all-in on beating Sovereign and Century." I tried to peg his tone, but I wasn't sure if it was quiet disappointment or a low rumble of accusation. "If your commitment is wavering—"

"I'm trying to find a way to beat him, okay?" I licked my still-dry lips. "I don't have the same powers as him. I'm not as old as him. The only thing I've got going for me at this point is that apparently he's got a case of puppy love that's keeping him from smearing me all over the Minneapolis skyline like ash in the wind. Give me some time." I kept calm, surprisingly.

"I don't have anyone better to take over for you," Foreman said, still terse, "so I don't see you going anywhere anytime soon. But don't make me regret this."

"If you do, it'll be too late," I said.

"You don't understand," Foreman said. "If it gets to that point, you'll be regretting it, too. Do you have any idea what sort of hell will be summoned forth if Sovereign unleashes some plan to enslave humanity? The United States Government isn't just going to lie down and dissolve quietly. They'll unleash every weapon at their disposal—chemical, biological, nuclear—to stop him." There was a silence. "You do realize that, right? You know that—"

"I know." I'd been through it all in my head. I knew what scared people were capable of when they got backed into a corner. I also knew that none of us had a clue what Sovereign had planned after metakind was wiped out. That part was still a big, gaping mystery. Less than one hundred metas against the combined might of every country in the world? Those weren't dynamite odds, even for someone as strong as Sovereign. After all, it wasn't like he was invincible. A good case of anthrax could still kill him. Probably.

"I just need to be sure your head is in the game," Foreman said. "You can't be chasing unrelated loose ends at a moment like this. Century is moving into the home stretch, and whatever their phase two is, it's months from being unveiled. We're close to the end, now."

I took a short, sharp breath, and it turned into a sigh. "I'm working on it. I just … I need one day here to wrap up this loose end, and I'll be back to sitting in Minneapolis, trying to figure out what to do next. Please."

The answer was a long time in coming. "You know what's at stake. You know what's coming for you, what'll happen to you if you lose. I don't expect you want to be a child bride for Sovereign, so I trust you'll do what you can to fight to the last." I could hear him pause, then sigh. "Because if you don't, what we unleash to stop him might just mean the end of humanity as well."

Chapter 18

I had hung up with him for only a moment when I realized the shower had stopped running. The door clicked open and Scott stepped out in nothing but a towel, still slightly dripping. I wondered why he even needed to shower when he could just spray himself with water, but I lost that question for some reason. Steam floated out into the room behind him.

"Sounded like a tense conversation," he said. He was just standing there, chest glistening. I don't know that my mouth was agape, exactly, but I'm pretty sure. "What little of it I caught at the end."

"What?" I blinked. Twice. "Oh, Foreman. Yes. Tense. He is … uhm … a little disturbed by our outing to Vegas."

Scott frowned. "How'd he hear about it?"

"Local PD called the FBI in Minneapolis, and I assume Li gave him a call immediately after. Because he's a super helpful guy like that."

"Nice," Scott said and started toward his overnight bag. I watched him. I couldn't help it, really. "Nice to know who the class tattletale is."

"It could have been Ariadne, I suppose." The towel was tight around his waist. Had he used a hand towel or was that my imagination?

"Maybe," he conceded. He knelt, and somehow the towel stayed on. It was like magic or something. Why couldn't I stop staring? This was … unsettling. Sort of. Maybe unsettling was the wrong word.

"What's next?" Scott glanced back at me. I snapped my eyes to meet his, but probably a few seconds too late. He smiled, and my face felt like it might burst into flames, Gavrikov-style.

"Uhmm, well," I said, full of wit and charm. And blushing. Lots of blushing. "I don't, ah … know."

"Are you checking me out?" he asked, a little coy. Not pouty, but … I don't know. Adjectives failed me. His chest was … really muscled. And shiny. Because of the water.

"I'm trying to keep my eyes above your collarbone," I said. Honestly I was.

"You're failing." Leave it to him to notice that. What a spectacular ass. Also, he was a jerk for pointing that out.

I pulled my gaze back to his face. "It's not my fault you're standing there all well-toned and … uh … wearing nothing but a towel." I took a breath. "Is this Caesar's Palace? Because I don't remember walking into a toga party."

He took a couple slow steps toward the bed. "I thought you were wrapped in barbed wire and coated in lemon juice?"

I cleared my throat. "You know I am. Which is why you should keep your distance."

He took a step closer, coming to the end of the bed. "Oh?"

Part of me wanted to remind him that he'd said we didn't have to discuss this until after Sovereign was dealt with. A very faint, fleeting part of me that I was trying desperately to find a metal box for, somewhere in my head. Too bad it didn't work that way for my own personality. "Yeah. My touch kills, remember? You wouldn't want to lose your soul."

He came up to the side of the bed where I lay and sat down on the edge. I went completely still, not even daring to breathe. His fingers went to my shoulder and slid down my sleeve to my good arm. It felt … um … "I'm not going to lose my soul doing that, am I?"

"Ah, no, but …"

He leaned over and kissed me, just for a second. His breath was fresh and minty and I knew for damned sure that mine was not. He broke after just a second. "Am I going to lose my soul by doing that?"

"Do enough of it and you might."

He leaned over me, his weight pressing me slowly to the bed. I could have thrown him off, easily, but I liked the feel of his bare chest against me. All the moisture was suddenly gone from his skin, and all I could feel was his warmth on top of me, bearing me down. He kissed me again, and I lost count of the seconds around three. He broke from me again and smiled.

"Your hand is on my ass," I said. It was. I could feel the gentle pressure he was applying through my clothes.

"I'm not going to lose my soul doing that, am I?"

Your hand, maybe, but not your soul, Zack threw up from somewhere within me. To Scott I said, "No," but I'm pretty sure my face betrayed me.

"What's wrong?" Scott asked.

"Nothing," I said. "We just … you know, there's a time limit on these sort of things, and you've already spent quite a few seconds of it." I didn't want to be too self-conscious because, honestly, I was enjoying myself. But at the same time, the specter of possible death hung over my every physical interaction, and it was always—ALWAYS—acutely on my mind.

He kissed me again, and I lost track of time again. When we broke he was still smiling. "What's the count?"

I blinked. "Hell if I know."

His smile grew wider. "Feeling like living dangerously?"

"It's your soul in peril, not mine."

"Yeah, but you'd have to deal with me in your head from now on." Why was he still grinning?

"After Wolfe and Bjorn, I think you'd be a picnic. On a summer's day. With ham salad."

His face creased. "Ham salad?"

I shrugged. "I like ham salad."

He started to lean in for another kiss but a buzzing filled the air. He froze, and we stayed like that for a moment, staring into each other's eyes until the realization hit me. I fumbled for my cell phone and looked at the faceplate. J.J. That little shit had a great sense of timing, that was for sure.

"Hello—"

I didn't even get to finish my sentence before he interrupted. "Hey, I got something on this search history that I think might be useful. Did you know there are a series of storm tunnels under the Las Vegas strip?"

I stared at Scott, whose face was still only inches from mine. Conscious of my bad breath, I tried to speak without expelling any air. The result was a very low, hushed answer. "No, J.J., I did not know that. Outside of the unlikely possibility that Weissman challenges me to a Loser-commits-suicide game of Trivial Pursuit, why should I care?"

"Because this guy—Antonio Morales? He was doing some hardcore research on those tunnels. Lots of searches, lots of page hits. Some YouTube videos, that sort of stuff. Everything else in his history was pretty generic, but this—I'm telling you, I think he's in the tunnels."

I pursed my lips and tried to speak without exhaling again. "You think he's in storm tunnels? Underneath us? Because … of his Google search history?"

There was a pause on the other end of the line. "Yep." The answer was self-assured. More self-assured than I would have been in his shoes, but my hushed voice was probably masking my irritation. "You should check it out."

I'm pretty sure I felt my eye twitch. "You think I should go crawling through sewer tunnels?"

"Storm tunnels," J.J. said. "Not sewer. There are a lot of homeless people living down there, apparently. You should see this YouTube video—"

"Thanks, J.J." I hung up the phone without saying anything else. Scott was still there, inches from my face, leaning toward me. I just stared at him, not really sure what I was thinking. "We should go check out the tunnels," I said and then promptly kicked my own mental ass for saying that.

Scott's face fell. "You want to go crawling through the sewers looking for this Antonio guy?"

I stared into his eyes. They were awfully pretty. "Want is a strong word. I think we need to do it. Then we can get on a plane and head home with a clear conscience."

He pulled up off me, back to the edge of the bed. He had been pressed up against me just a second ago, and the removal of his weight didn't leave me feeling any better. It felt worse, actually. "I'll get dressed," he said, and he was back to a neutral tone of voice.

He picked up his clothes and retreated to the bathroom. Part of me wanted to say something—anything. But instead I watched his towel-covered backside as he went into the bathroom and closed the door. And then I beat the hell out of myself for all the clever, exciting, sexy things that came to mind now that he was gone.

Chapter 19

It was hot. Sauna hot. Oven hot. Standing-next-to-a-bonfire-with-a-winter-jacket-and-flannel-pants-on hot. I sweated as I stared down the dark tunnel ahead. Pieces of garbage that had probably been washed out during the last rain were strewn all over the dusty ground. When was the last rain in this town? My money was on two decades ago.

We headed into the dark, a couple of flashlights we'd bought at a tourist shop our only guides. My current plan was to find a transient and offer him money in exchange for information. Insensitive? Probably. But I was hiking through a series of storm tunnels in the middle of the horrendous desert heat—and the shade? It didn't help as much as you might think, not today.

The place had a smell about it that made me wonder if I had wandered into the sewers by mistake. The air was a little more moist than it was outside, but still fairly dry, like a sub-zero day in Minnesota. My nose felt completely parched, like the skin inside was cracking the way my lips were. I was sweating as we continued down the concrete tunnel. Scott was at my side. I could tell by his flashlight beam and the occasional brush of his arm against mine.

"Quiet down here," he said. Our footsteps echoed softly as we walked.

"It was until you spoke," I said, hushed. My eyes were in constant motion. My dealings with Century had me expecting someone was going to come leaping out at us at any moment.

We hiked for a little while, dirt, grit and gravel all along the floors of the tunnel system. I could hear what sounded like dripping water every now and again, and we would occasionally find a puddle unexpectedly.

"I would have thought we'd see someone by now," Scott said.

"Probably avoiding us because they think we're cops," I said. The darkness, the slightly confined nature of the space—it was coming together to make me feel like I wanted to run. "You can see these lights a long way off in the tunnels, after all."

"How do you suppose someone ends up here?" Scott asked. "You know, living beneath the most extravagant resorts and casinos, where money flows like the water that comes through these drains. It's like a paradise of cash up there."

I tilted my light to look toward a dripping sound at my right. There was a damp spot and a small puddle on the ground. "The usual ways, I suppose. Bad luck. Economic setbacks. Maybe some of them have addictions to feed. I don't really know." The whole discussion gave me a feeling of deep discomfort. I really didn't know, and even speculating made me feel awkward and out of place.

"My dad always used to say mental illness, drugs, alcohol and bad choices," Scott said, never breaking his pace as he walked along. "Not the most empathetic guy." Scott paused. "Hey, did you hear that?"

I did. We both halted, waiting in the dark. I thought about turning off my flashlight, but instead I slowly scanned around us in a three-hundred-and-sixty-degree degree pattern until something moved, scaring the hell out of me.

"Gambling," came a rough, gravelly voice. I kept the light on the speaker, and he held up a hand to shade his eyes. "It's how I ended up down here."

"Jesus," Scott said. "You're a quiet one."

"I tapped my fingers so you'd know I was here," the guy said. I moved my light slightly to the side so it wasn't shining in his face anymore. "Didn't mean to startle ya. Awfully jumpy for a couple of well-dressed youths scouring through the tunnels. Who are you? Charity workers? College kids on a project?" His voice was rough, like sandpaper running over concrete.

"Looking for someone," I said.

"Found someone you have," he said, changing the pitch of his voice to sound like Yoda. "You guys cops?" he asked, with amusement.

I shined the light in my own face and held it there. "I look like a cop to you?"

"You look like a young girl," he said. I moved the light back over to him and saw he was wearing a plain wife-beater shirt that was a little grey from repeated washings. He had a beard yellowed from tobacco use and eyes that were squinted from years of looking at the sun, I suspected. He didn't look pale, at least not as pale as I did, which was interesting considering he lived underground. "But that doesn't mean you're not a cop. I used to watch those shows about the twenty-somethings they'd stick undercover in schools to catch the—"

"Whatever," I said with a sigh.

"Okay, you're a kid," he said. "What are you here for?"

"I told you, I'm looking for someone. A friend," I said. "Antonio Morales."

His squint got deeper. "Uh huh. You're a 'friend' who's looking for someone in the tunnels. Out of the goodness of your heart. Dressed in a suit jacket."

I glanced down. "I'm also wearing jeans."

"How grateful do you think your friend Antonio is going to be when you find him?" the guy asked. "Do you think he'd be grateful enough to pay me for showing you to where he may—or may not—be staying?"

"Probably not," Scott said after we exchanged a look. "Antonio … he's fallen on some hard times."

"Well, isn't that a familiar refrain." The guy didn't seem impressed. "All right, I might—or might not—know where he could be. I could show you the way, but you'll pay the cop rate."

"There's a cop rate?" Scott asked. "How much?"

"Five hundred," the guy said, his tanned face surrounded by the darkness. He grinned, a toothy grin.

"What's the non-cop rate?" Scott asked.

"Twenty bucks."

"Whatever," I said again, and pulled out my wallet. I counted out three crisp hundreds that I'd drawn from the cashier at the campus before I left. "You get the rest when we get there."

"I'm feeling like my rates should go up," the guy said as I put my wallet away.

"I'm feeling a bit of police brutality could be in your future," I replied, dour.

"You said you weren't cops!"

"And I thought you saw through my bullshit," I said and gestured with my flashlight. "Let's go."

"Wait," Scott said, "what's your name?"

"You can call me Grinder," the guy said. He stroked his yellowed beard as he spoke.

"If your mother named you that, someone should really give her a stern talking to," I said.

"Well, she's long dead, so I expect it'll sail right over her head," Grinder said, deadpan, "but you're welcome to try."

I could tell after about ten minutes that Grinder was the kind of guy who liked to fill every pause in a conversation. The funny thing was, he didn't really do it in the way I was used to. Most people who were like that tended to talk about themselves. Grinder, he went about it a different way.

"We're under the new City Center development right now," Grinder said. "Aria Casino, the Mandarin Oriental—"

"That's kind of a racist name nowadays, isn't it?" Scott asked.

"I think you're thinking of the Mandarin who's the Iron Man villain," Grinder said. "And that's more because he's a caricature of Asian stereotypes, you know?"

"He mixes things up a lot," I said. "Just earlier, he switched up Barry Allen with Barry Manilow."

"How can you not know the Flash?" Grinder said, shaking his head sadly. "It's like confusing Hal Jordan with Hal Holbrook."

Scott stayed quiet for a second. "I have no idea who either of those people are."

"We're almost there," Grinder said, his first bit of actual pertinent dialogue since he'd offered to show us to Antonio.

"Oh, yeah?" Scott asked. "Where's 'there'?"

"Here," Grinder said as he slid toward a side tunnel that had a curtain hanging by a rod that had been somehow nailed into the concrete. "Down this tunnel you'll find a few people sleeping on the floor."

"Sleeping?" Scott asked. "It's the middle of the day."

"We work at night," Grinder said, and I could see by the shadowed look on his face he took a little umbrage at Scott's observation. Scott, wisely, did not say anything to that. "The rest of the money?"

I pulled open my wallet and pulled two more hundreds out of it. I started to hand them to him and then yanked them back. Like an asshole, yes. "You told us you'd take us to Antonio."

"I said I'd take you to where he might—or might not—be staying," Grinder said. He was smiling again now. "You agreed, therefore you owe me the last two hundred."

"You could have led us into a blind, dead end with wording like that," Scott said. His voice told me his hackles were raised.

"And maybe I have," Grinder said, "but you still owe me two hundred dollars, at least based on our verbal agreement."

"Wow, a homeless contract lawyer," I said dryly. "Why don't we take a peek inside and if we find Antonio, you can have the rest of the money?"

Grinder gave that a moment's thought before he turned toward the curtain. "ANTONIO!" he bellowed, and it echoed through the halls. "COPS ARE HERE FOR YOU! BETTER GET RUNNIN', PAL!" With that, Grinder turned back to face us, almost apologetic. "Sorry. I was gonna warn him even if you paid. Can't live down here if we don't watch each others' backs."

"Son of a bitch," Scott said, and pushed Grinder neatly to the side. He ripped the curtain back, but there were already shouts and echoes in the chamber beyond. "There he goes!"

I flashed a look at Grinder and he shrugged again, almost apologetic. I tossed the two hundred bucks at him and took off at a flat run after the shadow of Antonio, already hauling ass down the tunnel way faster than any human would have been able to.

Chapter 20

"Antonio Morales!" Scott called. Our flashlight beams bounced wildly along the dark tunnel as we hurried to catch up with the fleeing man ahead of us. We were passing people on both sides, bedding spread on the floor of the tunnels, possessions scattered around the little stakes held by the owner of each bed.

Someone tossed something in my path, but I avoided it. I assumed we'd get more obstacles tossed in our way if the residents had more time. Something clattered in front of me short of my flashlight's beam and I neatly dodged it.

Scott did not.

I heard him hit the pavement, the wind leaving him in one giant, "OOMPH!" His flashlight hit the ground and rattled, the beam dancing over the graffiti-covered walls.

"You okay?" I tossed behind me.

"Keep going!" Scott said, and I could hear him a hundred feet back, pushing himself back to his feet. His flashlight beam was rolling in a slow circle now. "I'll catch up!"

I hit a ninety-degree turn and ran up the slope of the wall. I came back down to earth and pumped my arms. Every step was a fight between trying not to jump and still maintain optimal speed. It was a struggle sometimes.

"Antonio!" I called, and my voice echoed comically high down the tunnel ahead. "I'm here to help you!"

For whatever reason, he did not answer back. Probably wisely.

I saw light ahead. His shadow was highlighted against the sun. It was an opening to the outside. I wondered where it would take me.

He burst out into the daylight and cut left, out of my sight. I was only a hundred feet back now and had been gaining on him. I ignored my first instinct to pull my gun and hoped I wouldn't regret it.

I burst out of the end of the tunnel and immediately hooked left like I'd seen him do. I halted for just a second, trying to get my bearings.

Casinos stood tall on either side of me. I blinked back against the blinding light, and realized that the side of the Bellagio's tower stood before me. Someone was running, not that far ahead of me. I saw him look back, and that was all I needed.

It was Antonio.

I tore off after him and ended up on a lane. I could see the strip ahead, the Bellagio on my left. There were trees obstructing my running path, but I followed Antonio as he ran through the midday heat and onto Las Vegas Boulevard. He headed north toward Caesar's Palace.

The Bellagio fountains were blowing streams of water a hundred feet into the air, a Celine Dion song blasting out of the nearby speakers as my feet hit the sidewalk. It might have been a magical Las Vegas moment if I hadn't been running hard to catch a fleeing meta.

Antonio was tearing ass, running faster than even most of the metas I'd met. He threw a glance back at me, and there was pure terror written on his face.

I was gaining on him, but slowly. Pedestrians were in the way now, for both of us. I watched Antonio steer around a blond tourist wearing nothing but a bikini as I dodged some guy wearing a Chewbacca suit. That had to be the crappiest job of the day. Other than mine.

Then Antonio bumped into a guy with a sign that went flying into the air as the guy went down. Antonio went on, but the guy lay there on the street cursing after him. I read the sign on the ground as I passed: "For $20 you can kick me in the nuts as hard as you want."

Never mind; that guy probably had the worst job of the day.

We blazed down the sidewalk in front of Caesar's Palace. The crowds were starting to thicken, and we were pushing them out of the way left and right. I pirouetted around a stroller in a move that would have looked much cooler on a football field, while ahead of me, Antonio was crossing the driveway into Caesar's without regard for the traffic. He rolled across the hood of a BMW amid a bevy of horns.

I just leapt the road when I got to it. What was the point of being stronger than a human if you didn't use it?

We were coming up on Treasure Island and I was only twenty feet behind him. At ten, I could probably launch into a tackle that would get him. Probably. He looked like he was wearing down. The foot traffic wasn't working in his favor because he wasn't shoving them aside the way someone like Weissman would have.

He was being gentle. He was trying not to hurt people. It was a mark in the column for him, as far as I was concerned.

"Antonio!" I shouted. "I need to talk to you!"

This time he actually answered. "I won't let you kill me!"

"If I was trying to kill you, I would shot your ass blocks ago!"

"I'm not gonna let you take me!" Well, that answer wasn't much better.

"Don't be an idiot!" I shouted. I was close to the ten-foot mark, but I honestly wondered if a flying tackle would be a great idea at this distance. Waiting would be preferable. The hot wind whipped over my face, and the smell of coffee from a Starbucks ahead filled the air. "I just want to talk!"

That time he didn't say anything. I could see the corner of another street ahead of us. We'd already crossed two major roads without using the overpasses. I couldn't chance another, not the least of which was because of the traffic streaming across the intersection at high speed.

If Antonio didn't leap, he'd have to be hella lucky not to end up splattered on some cabby's bumper.

I was only six or so feet behind him now. I leapt and hit him in mid-back, sending him tumbling to the ground.

The world whirled around me. I hit my shoulder on the sidewalk and rolled out of it. I heard Antonio face-plant and roll then hit a trashcan. I felt a little bad about that.

I sprang back to my feet, feeling the shock of the jump run through my knees. There were aches and pains all over me—some from what I'd just done, some from what had happened in the casino fight earlier. The air smelled of car exhaust as I stood on the corner of Las Vegas Boulevard and stared at Antonio Morales as he pulled himself off the ground.

He looked younger than he had in the memory I'd pulled from Samuel. And taller. He unfolded himself, bracing against the trashcan, and stared at me with hard eyes. He stood there, slumped, for just a minute, breathing hard.

And then he pulled a gun out of his waistband and pointed it directly at me.

Chapter 21

I didn't hesitate before rolling to the right. It was pure instinct, a flashy move designed to disrupt his aim. I'd seen him stick an unsafetied gun in the front waistband of his pants; this was not a man used to handling firearms.

My suspicion paid off, apparently, and no gunshot rang out. I lost sight of him for a moment as I rolled, faster than any human could have. I angled myself toward him. Still no shot rang out and when I came out of my roll he was adjusting his aim toward me, a second behind.

Like an amateur.

I'd put myself close enough to be within leg's reach of him. For most people, this wouldn't have done them any good. Close for most meant point-blank range. An easy shot, easy kill.

For me, point-blank range meant I was close enough to sweep his leg.

And that's just what I did, kicking them from underneath him with only a little thought to mercy. I didn't break his ankles, though—and I could have—so mercy wasn't totally off the table.

He hit the ground and I rolled on top of him, getting a hand on the gun and twisting it to trap his finger in the trigger guard. It was a nice little Sig Sauer. The safety was still off, though, so I fixed that problem immediately.

"Ahhhhh," he said, making little noises of pain. His finger was at a very uncomfortable angle. "Please—!"

"I'm not going to hurt you," I said, using the gun's grip on his finger to twist his arm and turn him face down on the pavement. "But I'm not going to let you shoot me, either, Antonio."

"I know who you are," he said, and his words came out with

more than a few grunts of pain interspersed between them. If he tried to resist me, he'd lose a finger. Even for a meta, that'd ruin your day.

"You have no idea who I am," I said, and pushed him over. He didn't fight, to his credit. Probably out of fear for that finger. Pain is a powerful motivator. "I'm with the—well, with the government agency responsible for policing metas."

"Oh, yeah?" He was face down on the sidewalk now, and I was trying to decide whether to cuff him or not. If I did, it was only because I feared his belligerence, not because I really wanted to arrest him. He'd capped a Century operative in the head; while that may have been against the laws of the city of Las Vegas, it had looked like self-defense to my eyes.

"Yeah, but don't test me," I said, "you go into Treebeard mode and you'll need to regrow some limbs—litera—"

"Oh, ha ha," he said, face muffled against the pavement. "Like I've never heard that one before."

I cuffed him. I didn't really want to, but it was as much for his safety as mine. If he tried to run again, I'd have to chase him, and by this point I was tired and fed up enough to shoot him just to get it over with. I pulled the gun off his finger when I was done, but none of his tension dissolved as I finished.

The crowds surged around us. A few lookie loos stopped, taking cell phone videos of us. I flashed my badge. "FBI. I'm going to have to ask you all to step back, please." Most of them cooperated, save for a drunken guy with a beer flask that was almost as tall as me. I thought about pushing it, but I didn't need trouble right now. "Let's go talk over here," I said to Antonio, lowering my voice. I helped him to his feet and steered him toward the footbridge ahead.

I sighed. I'd recognized where we were but hadn't given it much thought. We were standing on the corner of Treasure Island's block, just across from the mall. I pushed Antonio gently along, his gun in my hand, and under the footbridge, I saw him glance at the broken concrete wall where Charlie had died. "Your handiwork?" he asked.

"No," I said quietly. "Someone killed my aunt right there."

I felt him tense. "It wasn't me—"

"I know it wasn't you," I said and leaned him against the wall a few feet from the place where it had happened. The heat was getting to me again, and I wished I could strip off my suit jacket. "It was Century, I think. The same people that came after you in the pawnshop."

"I know who they are," Antonio said with a slow nod and more than a little resentment.

"How?"

"They tried to recruit me," he said, dark eyes focused on the road ahead. The sounds of traffic seemed especially loud here under the pedestrian footbridge, and the shade provided did little to diminish the Vegas heat. All around us, the sun-lit streets were bright enough that I felt like I needed sunglasses, even here in the shade. "I declined."

"I don't know anyone else who's declined and lived to tell the tale," I said, keeping my hand fastened around his upper arm. "They're pretty persuasive."

"They have this woman," he said. "Short, kind of … well, chubby. She's a mind-reader. But she can't do anything to me when I'm even partially in tree form, because I'm not human, see?"

"You mean the one that was outside the pawnshop when the big guy came at you?"

"Yeah, her," Antonio said. "Claire or something."

"I met her yesterday," I said.

"How'd that go?" he asked, voice laced with irony.

"She's not going to be dancing anytime soon," I said. "I sent her off to our prison in the Arizona desert. Unconscious, so she couldn't cause anyone any problems." I glanced at him, and he seemed to be looking at me with guarded disbelief. "Listen, these guys—Century—they're killing everyone. All our people."

"I know," he said, nodding slowly. He looked away. "They came to me wanting help with that. Said if I killed for them, I could live, could be part of this … new order they were building. A new world." He looked back at me and the fear in his eyes was tangible. "Every word they said scared the shit out of me."

"How'd you get away?" I asked.

"That woman—Claire. Mind-reader? She was there, and she was supposed to tell the guy who came to talk to me what I was thinking." Antonio's shoulders were slumped. "When they confronted me, I went to tree form. You could see the panic in her face. She was whispering to the guy, telling him how she couldn't do a damned thing, couldn't read me. She was talking loud, her eyes all wide. You could see she was just … she didn't know what to do. I don't think she'd ever run across someone she couldn't … dominate before."

"What did they tell you?" I asked. "About what they were gonna do?"

"Take over the world," Antonio said, and now his eyes were mournful. "Kill a lot of people to make it happen. Build it better. Make sure they were unopposed. I got the feeling … that whatever they told me, it wasn't the same thing they told everyone. They guy doing the talking … Griswold, I think his name was? He seemed kind of stuttery. Like he didn't know what to say. Contradicted himself a few times, like he was telling me what I wanted to hear." Antonio shrugged, as much as a person in handcuffs could shrug. "I don't know. It all sounded like … like Nazi-concentration-camp stuff to me. Scary."

"Gah, there you are!" Scott's voice reached me. I looked toward the corner and saw him striding toward us. A few of the lookie loos who had filmed and watched us were still standing near the entrance to the footbridge, cell phone cameras still going. Probably hoping I'd deal Antonio a beating they could put on YouTube. "I've been—" He brushed against the guy with the huge beer flask. "Get lost, will you?" He flashed his badge. "Unless you want me to take you in for a toxicology screening." Beer flask took off. Scott made his way over to us. "He tell you anything?"

"A lot," I said, glancing at Antonio. "Not much we didn't already know." I reached down in my pocket and pulled my handcuff keys. "All right, Antonio, this is where we part ways."

I could feel the tension in his arms. "Part ways? Part ways how?"

"Wait, you're gonna let him go?" Scott asked me in near-disbelief. "He killed a guy!"

"A Century operative who had come to kill him," I said. "Sounds like a pretty clear-cut case of self-defense to me. What else should I do? Lock him in a cell in Arizona until Century comes for him there? Turn him over to the Vegas PD so he can cool his heels in a cell there until they come for him? Or he breaks out? Could be either." I stuck the key in his handcuffs. "I don't have the inclination to sentence him to death, Scott. Out here in the world, he's maybe got a chance. If he finds a new place to hide."

"You kinda blew my old place to hide," Antonio said with more than a little reproach. "I had it good down there."

"Claire was combing the hotels on the strip yesterday," I said. "I think she was sensing you, and she ended up running into us by mistake."

"Wait, what?" Scott's face was crumpled. "I thought Century sent that team after us!"

"I don't think so," I said with a shake of the head. "Maybe, but I don't think so. I think she got a read on Antonio and was trying to track him down. It just never occurred to her he was under the strip instead of in a hotel overlooking it. Then, when she caught a whiff of us, she tried to take you out. I mean, if they're out to kill all the metas, knocking one of the only ones still protecting them out of the game is a pretty good day's work, right?"

"They're not gonna stop," Antonio said as I let him loose from the cuffs. He rubbed his wrists, and I could see a little line where they'd rested. "They're gonna keep coming for me."

"Maybe," I said. "But their net is getting more holes in it by the day. We've taken over half their telepaths—mind readers—out of circulation. We've killed about a tenth of their operatives, total. We get a few more, it's going to put a hell of a dent in their ability to track people down. I'm pretty sure it already has."

Antonio looked at me with shadowed eyes. "You're really serious, aren't you? You're … actually fighting them."

"I've gone toe to toe with them more times than I can count lately," I said with a sigh. "And I'll keep going until either they get knocked down for the last time or I do."

Antonio nodded, just barely, like he was still considering something. "You're really gonna let me go?"

I waved my hand toward the street. "Go plant yourself somewhere safe, but don't put down roots." All that was pure smartassery. I softened my tone. "And I wish you the best of luck."

He took a couple steps away, like he was testing to see if I was lying. I watched Scott. His face was red, like he couldn't believe I would let Antonio walk. But I did.

And he made it all the way to the corner before he turned back around.

"4627 Eagle Hill Terrace out in Henderson," Antonio said. He stood at the corner, a little standoffish. He was almost merged into a crowd. As if it gave him a feeling of security.

"What's that?" I asked, a little confused.

"It's where they talked to me about joining them," he said. "It's where I fought my way out. I think it's their base or whatever here in town." People were passing in front of him now. "Good luck to you, too," he called, and I saw him turn, heading south along the strip. I watched him disappear from where I stood under the footbridge, and he vanished into the wash of tourists.

Chapter 22

"We clear on what's going to happen here?" I asked Scott as he parked the car two doors down from 4627 Eagle Hill Terrace. The brakes squeaked and the car shuddered as he slid it into park before it was fully stopped. The AC was blasting full in my face until he killed the ignition, at which point silence filled the cabin.

"Yeah," Scott said, voice filled with tension. I could almost hear it quiver. "We're going to roll up into this place like gangsters and gun down anything that moves."

I frowned at him. I wasn't sure if he was joking, but I let it slide and threw open my door. A wave of Vegas heat hit me in the face. "Such a smartass." He didn't sound happy, but then, who would be given what we were about to do?

"I know, we're well matched." There was a hint of tension in his voice that was different than I'd heard before from him. I would have asked him about it, but this wasn't really the time.

I opened the back door of the car and reached down into the floorboard. We'd made a quick stop-off after we'd gotten the tip from Antonio. I was impressed with how helpful and friendly the manager of a Vegas gun store had been when we'd shown him our FBI badges and mentioned we were heading into a raid on a house where they were suspected to stock heavy firepower.

Really heavy firepower. It was the honest truth.

He hadn't even asked us why we didn't call in a SWAT team. He'd just showed us the weapons that weren't available to the general public and made sure to check our credentials with the local field office before we'd walked out the door with a couple of choice weapons. We paid, of course, which might have been the wellspring of his generosity of spirit, but I had no complaints.

Money greased wheels. I had money, and I had wheels that needed greasing.

And as I placed the stock of the AA-12 fully automatic shotgun against my shoulder, I had a suspicion it was more than wheels that were about to get greased.

Scott matched me on the other side of the car, an AA-12 of his own against his shoulder. I nodded to him and we shut the doors quietly. I'd already made a call to the Henderson PD informing them that we had probable cause to search the house, and they had been polite enough to offer to send a couple units out as backup. Which I'd accepted, but told them to wait ten minutes. Not sure quite what the dispatcher thought of that, but hey, she wasn't paid to think.

We walked side by side down the boiling sidewalk, and I wondered if anyone was calling the police on us right now. That was the whole reason I'd called the Henderson PD, as a hedge against that sort of trouble. Now I had ten uninterrupted minutes to sweep through this house of Century's before I had to deal with backup, and I planned to use my time wisely.

"You sure we should be doing this?" Scott asked as we made our way up the walk. His voice betrayed him, all shot through with uncertainty.

"Wiping out our astounding number of enemies? Yes." I ignored the fact that Scott's objection might be moral in nature and focused solely on the immediate problem at hand.

"Okay," Scott said with a cringe that hinted he might not share my confidence. "You want me on the back door or front?"

"Front," I said, and my feet clacked against the rocky lawn as I stepped off the path. "Give me thirty seconds and then kick down the door."

"Shame we don't have any breaching rounds," he murmured and braced himself just outside the front door.

"Like you need a shotgun to open a door," I muttered as I turned the corner of the house. I wasn't being as quiet as I wanted to be because I was hunched over and moving quickly to get into position. I knew that any meta worth their salt would hear me outside the window, but because I was hunched over, they wouldn't be able to see me even if they looked out.

Part of that was strategic, too. If they heard someone moving toward the back door, they'd be paying attention to it when the front door got kicked in. That should allow me to take the focus off Scott and put it on me.

Which meant—lucky me—I'd have the highest probability of dying during this raid. But that's the way it should have been, in my view. I wanted to be the lightning rod. I'd seen too many people who deserved to live die instead of me. Andromeda. Zack. Breandan.

I crouched outside the back door, my back against the hard, puckered stucco wall. The ridges were poking me, little lines etching into my skin. I was doing a mental countdown in my head, and I only had five seconds to go.

Five …

Four …

Three …

At two, I took a deep breath and let it out slowly. Even though I knew I was the lightning rod, even though I wanted to draw the attention of everyone in the house to me, I was still scared.

I got to my feet and faced the back door. It looked like a hollow-core, like something you'd use to seal off a bedroom rather than protect the exterior of your house, and I started to wonder if Century gave even half a damn about their own security.

Or maybe they weren't worried because no one but me was crazy and stupid enough to come after them.

I kicked the door down with one well-placed heel. It crashed inward and I was through in a second. I swept my shotgun left, then right, placing my back against the wall and looking into a kitchen.

A man was waiting just inside, cup of coffee in his hand. He clearly hadn't heard my approach, because his face went from blank to rage in a half-second. I hesitated, holding off on pulling the trigger until he said, "Sienna N—"

I pulled the trigger and opened up on him with two rounds of double-ought buck to the torso and head. His face and chest exploded in a blast of red. I heard the front door come crashing down, followed by the repetitive, heavy booms of Scott's shotgun in action.

Once I was sure the corners were clear in the kitchen, I spared only a look to make sure my target was dead. He was; even a meta couldn't survive having their skull emptied. I swept down the hall and broke left, kicking open a door to a bedroom.

The whole place was yellow, from the paint on the walls to the sheets on the bed. There was a woman sitting up in the bed, eyes locked on me as I came through the door. My world started to blur and I stroked the trigger instinctively.

The yellow walls turned red and the world around me returned to normal, her telepathic influence ended. Red streaks dotted the yellow paint and yellow sheets, and once I'd confirmed the room was clear, I left the body where it lay and moved on to the next room.

I caught a glimpse of Scott coming out of a door at the far end of the hall. "Living room and master bedroom are clear. This is the last one," he said.

"Let's get this over with," I said, gritting my teeth as I kicked the door open. It broke neatly in half and flew inward.

My gun was up before I'd even registered that there were three people in the room. One of them started to raise a hand, and my subconscious moved the shotgun into alignment and peppered him with three shots from a single stroke of the trigger. He splattered and fell, and I moved to the next target.

This one was another woman, bulkier than most. She reminded me a little of Eve, save for the fact she was shorter. She had a hand up as well, but she had hesitated, her eyes glazed. Something flew at me. I dodged right and unloaded on her as well, splotches of red exploding from her midsection and chest.

I took aim at the last target and halted. It was a man, sitting on a chair in the middle of the room. I pulled my finger off the trigger and lowered my weapon.

"What the hell was that?" Scott asked from just outside the door. I glanced back and saw the wall opposite the door burned black from the heat of whatever sort of power the woman had heaved at me. If I'd been standing there when it came through … I shuddered.

"Room's clear," I said, staring at the man in front of me. He stared back and nodded, gentle eyes sizing me up. His face was worn, bruised and bloodied. His hands were tied behind his back, his legs were secured to the metal chair by heavy chains.

I saw Scott pop his head in behind me. "What…the…f—"

"Now, now," the man said in a deep voice, soothing as any I'd ever heard. "There's no need for that kind of talk, Scott."

"What the hell are you doing here?" Scott asked, jaw somewhere around his ankles. Mine should have been, too, but somehow I was unsurprised.

"I'm a prisoner of Century," the man said, rattling the chains. "Isn't it obvious? They've been using my … unique skills … to aid them in their mission. It would seem they're running a bit low on internal talent for …" he glanced at me and smiled, "… some reason."

I took a step closer to him, still sitting in the chair as if all was well. Some of his bruises and cuts were fresh, others looked like they'd been there a while. Probably not something they'd started when they heard me crashing through the back door. "I didn't think I'd ever see you again."

"Well, if I'd had it my way, you wouldn't have," he said with a slight chuckle. "But Century caught me as I was about to flee the country. It would appear there is no safe ground when it comes to them." His face darkened. "Or Sovereign."

"No," I said, "there's really not."

"So, what's it to be?" he asked, as though he were awaiting nothing more than a minor decision. "Your options are somewhat limited, of course, but I'm quite at your mercy."

"Find the key to his chains," I said to Scott, "let's cut him loose."

Scott looked at me like I was crazy. I noticed his hand shook on the fore grip of his shotgun. "Umm … Sienna …"

"Do it," I said, turning my eyes back to the man in the middle of the room.

"Do you not remember when he—"

"I remember everything," I said, staring at the warm eyes that stared back at me. I wondered if he was in my head even now, moving things around to his liking. For some reason, I suspected … not. "After all, it'd be awfully hard to forget someone like Dr. Zollers."

Chapter 23

It took a little while to iron things out with the Henderson PD at the scene. After all, we'd left ten bodies in the house, and that wasn't exactly a normal thing for a raid. I'd called Li as soon as it was done, and he'd immediately whistled up the chain to his superiors in the FBI to help cover it for us. I figured he'd be pissed, but he didn't give me an ounce of trouble. I counted my blessings on that one.

When the Henderson PD cleared us to leave the scene, they didn't even confiscate our shotguns. Which was a plus. Zollers was remanded to our custody without argument. I wondered just how big a dick the FBI was swinging on my behalf; I suspected that being backed up by Foreman and whomever he had on his side in the Senate wasn't hurting a bit.

It took about two hours for us to get clear, and by the time we were done, I was famished and had to go to the bathroom. We rode in silence until we pulled off at a place called In and Out burger. It was well past the dinner hour by now, and even if I had adjusted to Pacific Time—which I hadn't—I would have been starving.

The smell of burgers hit me in the face as we walked in. We ordered once I'd made my pit stop, still not speaking. Zollers was quiet, which was kind of par for the course for him, and we sat down in a booth while we waited for them to call our number.

Scott was the first to speak, and what he said surprised me. "What the hell did we just do back there, Sienna?"

I glanced at Zollers, who arched his eyebrows slightly as if to say, "You should have expected this." I hadn't, though. "What do you mean?" I asked. I knew what he meant, but I needed a second to prepare my defense.

"Are you kidding me?" Scott leaned in, speaking in a hushed tone. "We just executed ten people. No trial, no due process, no nothing."

I kept my expression neutral. "And?"

Zollers kept absolutely silent. Scott's eyes bulged. "That. Was. Murder."

"Probably," I agreed, keeping emotion out of it. I tried to remember if I'd ever argued the line between murder and killing before, and decided that if I had, it was probably in my head. Or with Old Man Winter, which made it irrelevant.

"Probably?" Scott's face was flushed red as a fresh strawberry. "We took shotguns in there and shot up the place."

"And you knew that's what we were going to do when we kicked in the doors," I said. I *should* have expected this. "You've killed people before, haven't you?"

The anger on his face dissolved, the redness abated, and his lower lip quivered. "Not like this." I saw a slight shudder run through his frame. "It was ..."

"What about the guys in the casino this morning?" I asked. "That didn't seem to bother you. You even got kind of ..." I reddened this time, knowing that Zollers was probably reading what I was thinking, "... feisty with me afterward."

"It was self-defense," Scott said, the emotion now bled out of his face. "They came at me. It was obvious they meant to kill me. They took you down—"

"They were the same people," I said. Now I had my thoughts organized. "The exact same people, from the exact same place. The ones who attacked us in the casino would have been right there at that safehouse later tonight if we hadn't killed them." This was true. Scott had killed four people in the front room as he entered, and the floor had been covered with inflatable mattresses—enough to sleep our attackers at the casino, when coupled with the beds in the rest of the house.

"But they weren't there," Scott said. "And they didn't attack us—"

"Yes, they did," I said. "Look, I get your argument. You want us to execute warrants, play by the rules, by the book." It was a funny thing for me to say to him, because truthfully, Scott had never been a by-the-book guy. I think we'd found his line this afternoon, though, and crossed right over it at high speed. "You want to try and convict these people, these Century operatives, and send them to jail in Arizona."

"No!" Scott said, and he was flushed again. "I get that things are different, okay? That we're not even subject to regular laws in the best of times, which these aren't—"

"We're at war," I said, like it ended the argument. It didn't, but it stopped him in his tracks. "This isn't just criminal behavior. They're not perpetrating a normal series of crimes. They're committing mass murder of an entire race in anticipation of conquering another one. Laws don't quite cover this. Simple treason doesn't fit the scope of their plans, and murder charges in a courtroom do a disservice to the epic nature of their evil.

"They mean to put a boot on our necks and squeeze the life out of us," I said. "Quietly, where no one can hear us struggle or scream. Where no one has the power to stop it, outside the realm of human laws. You want a black and white world where we can live by the laws? I'm here to tell you that you're going to drown in the grey. This isn't law and order and justice for all mankind. This is survival. This is the law of nature—a pack of wolves who are going to eat you in the dark of night, and you can either shoot them first or get devoured. Your choice."

Scott listened to me unload without stopping me in the middle, and I could see the warring emotions on his face. His hand shook as he picked up his water cup, and he fumbled it before putting it back on the table. "It felt wrong, Sienna. Just wrong."

"What would you suggest we do instead?" I asked.

"Overwhelm them with all our people," he said without waiting a moment. "Raid them without going in and blowing them to pieces without warning. Cuff them and send them off to Arizona to cool off under the desert until we had them all—"

"Conveniently in one place?" I asked. "Where Sovereign can get them all at once?"

"Like we did with that telepath, Claire," Scott said. His voice sounded stronger than he looked. "That was righteous. That was—"

My phone buzzed, loudly, and he stopped talking. I pulled it out and checked the number. It was my mom. I accepted the call. "Hello?"

"Well, you got the 'hell' part right," she said. Mom was always tense, but right now she sounded tenser than usual.

"What happened?" I felt a sick drop in the pit of my stomach, and I stood involuntarily, knocking my knee against the edge of the table as I got up. They'd come. Finally. They had to have—

"Century just hit our prison facility in Arizona," she said. "And they left a lot of dead bodies in their wake."

Chapter 24

We were headed south on US 93. Our prison facility was outside Phoenix, which according to the GPS was less than five hours drive. Quicker than trying to get a flight. Scott had us going about a hundred miles an hour, and Li had warned local law enforcement that we were coming through in a civilian vehicle and not to mess with us. That was convenient, I had to admit.

Zollers was in the back, still keeping his silence. Scott had been quiet for the last few hours as well. We'd hurried to eat our burgers—which were amazing, by the way—before running out the door. There wasn't really any reason to hurry; the facility was utterly destroyed according to the one person we'd had on the scene.

We didn't have any metas on duty in the prison, because we didn't have any to spare. The Directorate had employed a few low-level meta guards, but they had died when Omega had hit the place.

But we didn't have very many prisoners, either, which meant meta guards weren't as necessary.

The dry desert stretched all around us, or at least I thought it did. It was night, and darkness shrouded everything. Stars gleamed down from overhead and the high beams of the rental gave us enough light to see by. There were taillights ahead of us in the distance, and every once in a while Scott would skirt around someone at high speed. There was not much traffic at this time of night.

Not much scenery, either. I was surprised at the level of foliage at the side of the road. There was a constant string of dry, brushy trees with branches jutting out, lit by our headlights. After we'd come down from some mountainous driving, I'd expected flat, empty desert. I hadn't seen it yet, though. I saw a surprising amount of green in the headlights. More than I would have thought, which would be none.

We passed through a town called Wickenburg, and I wondered why we were even bothering to come down here. We'd heard the report; the prison was destroyed. I would have said leveled to the ground, but it was already underground.

"Maybe we'll find something there," Zollers said, breaking a silence that had lasted for umpteen hours now.

I turned to face him in the back seat. "Do you really think so, or are you just telling me what I want to hear?"

He shrugged and offered a weak smile. "Probably the latter. I am more than a little indebted to you, after all."

I turned back to the view of the headlights falling over the brush on the sides of the highway. "Enough to want to join the fight?"

"Well, let's not go crazy or anything," Zollers said dryly. "By my rough estimation and bearing recent events in mind, you're still overmatched on the order of something along the lines of eight to one."

"Well, it was easily ten to one when we started, so at least we're getting closer," I said tautly. Scott said nothing, but I detected a noticeable flinch where he was hunched over the wheel.

"Yes, but every one you lose is worth more to you than seven of theirs," Zollers said. "I'm just going to point this out to you—the moment they remove your support system, you are effectively finished."

I pursed my lips, hard. "I know that."

"I don't think you do." His polite tones were even more irritating than his accurate points. "I think on a cerebral level, you recognize that without this new cobbled-together Agency, you'd be in over your head. I think on a gut level, though, you're in a state of pure reaction."

"Stop the car," I said, and Scott shot me a look like I was crazy. "Pull over. Now."

He did, bringing the car to a gradual, coasting stop. Zollers obliged me, not saying anything else until we were on the side of the road. I started to tell him to get out, but he did it without me having to open my mouth. "Wait here," I said to Scott, and opened the door to follow Zollers out into the desert.

The night was still damned warm, and my feet sunk slightly in the sand, like I was walking on a beach. Zollers led the way, the shadow of his form guiding me into the desert. We walked a hundred feet off the road before he stopped, probably sensing I wanted some distance from Scott for this. It wasn't that I didn't trust him, it was that … I didn't want him to hear what came next.

"What do you know?" I asked.

"Not much more than you," Zollers said. He watched me calmly, hands in his pockets. He pulled them out and showed them to me, open-handed, and it took me only a second to realize my naturally suspicious nature had caused me to think he might be holding a weapon before I'd even had a chance to verbalize anything. "But I've met Sovereign, and I have a sense of the man. I've met Weissman, and I know he's a snake. Sovereign won't let him hurt you, directly, but Weissman will come after your support mechanism with everything he has."

"He hasn't done it yet," I said, jutting my chin out in defiant pride.

"You haven't been a big enough pain in his ass until just now," Zollers said. "That Omega operative—Hildegarde? She was a bigger thorn in his side until recently. When word got out in the safe house about what you did in Florida to their telepaths, there was this sense of palpable dread. I get the feeling you weren't considered a problem until then. Now, you're bound to be priority one."

"How did the people in Vegas know about what happened in

Florida?" I asked.

Zollers sighed. "Something you need to understand about your enemy—they are on offense, not defense. The reason you've been so effective in your last few moves is that they're attacking, not countering you. They're set up to destroy, and very little thought was given to what you would call operational security. The idea that they could be attacked, that they would even be visible to their enemies ... I don't think Weissman saw it coming, and I'm not sure that with the hundred people he had at his disposal he could even cover that risk."

"So he's vulnerable," I said. "They're vulnerable."

"They're only vulnerable so long as you're still a threat," Zollers said, and I could tell he was cautioning me. "You're the *only* threat to them. If a SWAT team had crashed down their doors, with human reflexes instead of your meta ones, Century's people might—maybe—have suffered one or two deaths, but the rest would have swept through that team and escaped. They were not prepared for *your* response. Don't be so arrogant as to think that they're not nearly invulnerable to anyone else's. Short of sending in the National Guard, their independently operating units are going to be nearly impossible to crack for anyone short of a meta team."

"But we could take them," I said, pondering.

"*If* you know where they are and *if* you catch them flatfooted like you did here—keeping in mind that they'll be expecting you from here on out—and *if* you don't run into any of their heavier hitters. I know this going to come as a surprise to you, but they have more powerful metas at their disposal. You've been dealing with the B-team, thus far. There are others as powerful as Weissman further up the chain."

I rubbed my chin. I felt like I'd been punched in it, even though it'd really just been a shock of awakening. I hadn't considered the possibility that I'd been dealing with the second stringers so far.

Century had seemed like such a black box, an impenetrable mystery, that I just took for granted that they were all about as powerful as the ones they'd thrown at us thus far. What else could they possibly have that would be worse than Loki? He was one of the old gods, after all. He'd lived for thousands of years, survived countless wars …

… and was scared stiff of Century. Scared enough to kill himself rather than face their wrath.

"I see you're coming to logical conclusions," Zollers said.

"Get out of my head." There was a quiet despair in the way I said it; even I could hear it.

"I'm afraid I can't," Zollers said, still holding his distance. "It's not something I can just turn off. The more forceful your thoughts, the more they jump out at me. And your thoughts, especially lately, are like shouts during a quiet night."

"Why?" I asked. He looked … troubled. Which I would have been, were I him.

He sighed again. "Because I'm entirely too fond of you." He shrugged, throwing his arms wide as if he couldn't explain it away. "I've counseled more people in the course of my duties than … well, there were a lot. Why do you stick with me? Why do I keep finding myself prodding your mind even after we parted ways? If I said I don't know, I'd be lying."

He took a step closer to me. Arms reach. I bristled, unseen, but I knew he knew it. "You're the only one who's going to fight, Sienna. You and that senator on your side, you're the only ones who would stand up and look Sovereign head-on and spit in his face." His expression wavered. "For a long while after the last time we met, I feared I was going to die. For a while, I was given a reprieve by Sovereign himself. Then Weissman came after me and forced me to do his will." He waved north, back the way we came. "After that, I knew I was going to die again. So, if I'm going to die—and it is almost certainly assured, regardless of whether you win or lose …" He smiled. "Then I might as well go out quickly, and fighting for something that matters, in the company of the only people who are actually going to fight."

Chapter 25

The prison site was a disaster area. Sand kicked up in the night wind and swirled to and fro, without any discernible pattern. I stood by the car and watched it go, a little tornado of dust caught in the headlights of the car. It was better than looking at the alternative.

The prison was a hole in the ground. I mean, I'd heard it was a hole in the ground from anyone who had ever described it to me, but that was semi-exaggeration. Built into the hollowed-out core of an old missile silo, the Directorate prison had originally had a building over it.

That was gone now. It looked like it had been corrugated metal at one point, like a warehouse. Pieces of it still remained, and the swirls of sand were playing over them. It might have been beautiful if it wasn't another sign of the inevitable calamity heading our way.

"They didn't really leave much, did they?" Scott asked. We were all standing by the car, ignoring the heat. I had a flashlight in one hand, my shotgun on a strap around my neck.

"Sure they did," Zollers said dryly. "They left a lot of wreckage."

"Helpful."

"Well, I know you don't just keep me around for my looks," Zollers said. "Figure my observational skills are a nice icing on the cake."

"Stow it, you two," I said, steeling myself. I didn't really want to descend into the earth. I could see the hole, and was hoping that the stairs that led down the silo were still intact. I had my doubts.

"Someone's touchy," Scott said, with a lot more grump than

usual. I glanced at him and noticed he didn't have his shotgun.

"You gonna go down there unarmed?" I asked.

"Yep," Scott said.

I stared hard at him for a minute. "Okay." I didn't waste another minute, just started toward the waiting hole.

"Well, I'd like a gun if he's not going to carry one," Zollers said, a rising note of concern. "But I suspect you want me to prove myself a little more before you arm me," he finished, taking the words right out of my mouth.

I approached the dark, shadowy hole in the ground. There was concrete around the edges of it, but it was already covered in a layer of desert sand. I went toward it, and took a look back to make sure they were still following me. Every step I took left footprints in the sand that had accumulated. Zollers was a few steps back; Scott was immediately behind me.

I was trying to decide how much I wanted to lay into Scott. I sensed he was fragile, and this probably wasn't the moment. Still, if he was so emotionally tipsy he didn't want to carry a gun into a situation where we had a definite danger … "What's the matter with you?" I asked. "Did you leave your common sense back in Nevada?"

"It's pronounced Ne-vad-uh," Zollers said. He shrugged. "You said Nev-AH-duh." I shot him a glare. So helpful.

"No, but I left a lot of bodies back there," Scott returned. "A lot of blood on the wall, a lot of brains. I'm not an assassin, Sienna. I'm not a killer."

"I am," I said, but it was a whisper. "If that's what it takes."

I was focused ahead now, shining a light into the pit in front of me. It was about fifteen or twenty feet in diameter, and my flashlight beam bounced down the shaft. I had my pistol out; I couldn't use my light and my shotgun at the same time. If only I'd had a Picatinny rail with a mountable light …

I wondered how many other nineteen-year old girls had *that* thought running through their mind. Probably very few. Hopefully fewer still if it involved sticking their head into a lion's mouth like I was about to do. I felt the quiver of fear and buried it. I hoped that me doing this—fighting this war, battling with my own fear—would keep a thousand, a million, a hundred million others from having to.

I shook my head and rested my first foot on the first metal step of the staircase that led into the shaft. It squeaked but felt firm, so I took the next. My light bounced, but everywhere I pointed it, the pistol swung with it. I braced my gun hand with the flashlight hand, crossing my forearms.

Every step brought a squeak of the staircase. I led the way, not bothering to check if Zollers and Scott were still behind me. They could have both chickened out and said they wanted to stay in the car and I'd still have had to do this. It wasn't like I could just give up, after all.

This was my baggage, and I'd picked it up long before I got back to Minneapolis.

We descended a whole floor before things widened out. There was a solid metal door ahead. It was partially open, and I crept around, keeping my gun pointed in front of me. The flashlight beam played off the walls and illuminated something against the back of the cell. It took my eyes and brain a minute to decode what I was seeing.

It was a body.

I thought I recognized the guy. I shined the light on his face and kept it there. I'd seen him in a file, something I'd gotten toward the beginning of my tenure in the new Agency. We'd considered trying to recruit some of the hard cases we had imprisoned here, adding them to the team to help fight Century and Sovereign. I'd pored over files in an effort to find some people worth saving.

I'd given up fairly quickly.

When Omega had hit the prison, the surface building had been blow up in one big damned hurry, doing more than a little damage to the upper levels of the prison, which—at the time—had hosted the less dangerous, less nasty/scary/vicious/murderous offenders. They were the ones who might actually have gotten out someday. Maybe.

Those floors had been destroyed in the explosion. Something about the pressure of the downward force of the bomb. I couldn't pretend to fully understand the physics of it, but it was a chaotic sort of mess, as I understood it. The only survivors had been the guys—and one woman—in the depths of the prison.

There were five of them. Five of the nastiest, most horrific criminals I could imagine. They would have fit right in at ADX Florence, the U.S. Government's Supermax prison in Colorado. They'd done things that were insanely disgusting, disturbing—premeditated attacks on people that were so violent and horrific that even I found them repellent.

Which took some doing, since I had the crown prince of all serial killers in my head and had perpetrated more than a few acts of violence in my day. Some of them more necessary than others.

The face of the man against the wall—he was one of those chosen few. Edgar something-or-other? Whatever. I approached his corpse slowly, just to be sure. I put a hand on his neck, pistol cocked all the while. I could deliver a bullet to his skull faster than he'd be able to grab at me.

I held my position there for a minute. There was no pulse, and his flesh was cold.

"There's no one alive here," Zollers said coolly.

"You don't know that," I said, pulling my hand back from Edgar Dead-gar's neck. "There could be an empath screening them."

"No," Zollers said with a shake of his head. "I can get a reading from a dead body for a little bit after the death."

"How does that work?" Scott asked.

"It's sort of like how you can see when you push your eyelids almost closed," Zollers said. "I can't read their mind anymore; there's just too much brain damage. But I get a vague sense that there were thoughts there once, as the neural activity fades. It's a radar ping, that's all. Enough to tell me there was someone there, once upon a time."

He took a breath in through his nose and then snorted. The stale prison air was dank and carried all the charming scents that followed a newly-dead body. Not the sort of things you would usually get a whiff of in a rose garden, that's for sure. Unless they had just laid down fertilizer.

"All right," I said. "We should head down. There's a guard post three levels in—"

"Why was this guy up top?" Scott asked. His eyes were squinted, like he was thinking. "Weren't the most dangerous criminals housed in the bottom of this place?"

"Yeah," I said, and my voice was taut. "When we rebuilt it after Omega's attack, I had them change it."

"Why?" Scott asked.

I sighed and hoped he wasn't going to get sensitive on me. "Because we knew Century was coming, and I suspected they'd use a bomb to force entry. I figured if they did, I wanted the worst of the worst to get pulped so that our jailers wouldn't have to worry about them escaping."

He just stared at me. "That's cold."

I shrugged. "I'm cold. I'm running a war, not a tea party, okay? I have to worry about what happens if murderous lunatics with insane powers escape into the outside world. Feelings and empathy don't get a lot of attention when I'm juggling concerns like that."

"Yeah, but—"

"No buts," I said. "It didn't matter anyway."

He looked like he wanted to argue, but he held his tongue.

"Why didn't it matter?"

I glanced to my right. "Because Century didn't kill this guy with an explosion."

Scott frowned. "What? They blew up the building up top, and—"

I shook my head and stopped him. I decided a visual would be more instructive, so I reached over and pushed Edgar's corpse over. He sagged, twisted, and fell stiffly face-down on the ground. Blood stained the wall and his back, where a gaping wound revealed broken ribs and a heart that had been ripped asunder.

Scott gagged. I stepped past him while he did and continued down. He caught up with me about the time I reached the guard station, Zollers trailing behind him. I suspected the doctor's "soft skills" when it came to being nice and dealing with people were more useful in comforting him than anything I could say. "How did you know?" Scott asked as he caught up with me. I could feel him at my shoulder, like he was breathing down my neck. Not in a good way.

"Century didn't blow up the building up top from the outside," I said. "They did it from the inside, as they left. And not with an explosive, either, but with something else. Maybe a windkeeper like Reed. The door to Ed's cell was opened from a guard station, not blown open. In short, this was another extermination, not an Omega-style retaliation with a bomb."

I could hear the gears turning in his head. "And you know all that just from looking?"

I didn't know quite what to say to that. "It seemed obvious to me from what I saw."

Whatever else he was going to say, he didn't, because we'd reached the guard station. The door here was opened, too. It didn't look forced at all; none of them had.

I pushed it on its hinges and it squeaked, alerting anyone left in the silo to our position. I cringed, but ultimately, I supposed it didn't matter. Assuming Zollers was right. Which I didn't assume, ever. I'd been caught flatfooted too many times to not keep my gun out.

I ran my light across the walls. There were dead guards everywhere; it had been an extermination all right, just the same as if someone had run across a den of rats. They were all dead, all over, and it hadn't even been a contest. I stepped over three corpses to make my way to a bank of monitors. None of them were operable, but I knew that the security apparatus was in here somewhere.

"Must have lost the backup power, too," Scott said. His voice still had an edge to it. "I think I can access the security system footage on my phone if you give me a few minutes."

I looked at the bodies strewn across the floor, figures shrouded in the dark. "We've got nothing but time."

I stood there in the silence, back against the wall while Scott searched the console for a data card. I watched him all the while, dimly recalling something J.J. had said about how on-site data dumps onto local storage. Where once they might have used a CD, now they used the little HD cards everybody put in their cameras and cell phones. Zollers found a whole box full of them in a nearby closet while we waited.

When Scott finally found it, he made a big show of plugging it into his phone. I couldn't really fault him for it; I suspected I knew how he felt. It was a heady feeling, killing the way we had at that safe house. Ones I'd done like that still haunted me. Parks's face showed up a lot in my nightmares. The bloody bubbles that had rushed up when I'd killed Clyde Clary. Eve Kappler's face as I drained her had been particularly accusing. Rick, the head of Omega, that had been … it had been …

I ran the back of my wrist over the bone at the center of my eyebrows, pushing it there like I could use it to relieve a headache. I didn't really have a headache, but thinking about all the people

I'd killed made me want to forget it all.

The ones after Rick … those I barely felt. Was it because they'd all happened in the course of defending myself or others? Or had I just calloused my soul to the point I didn't notice anymore? Scott had no such callousing.

"Okay," Scott said, concentrating on his phone. I felt pity for him as he worked. "I think I've got it."

I shuffled toward him, avoiding the bodies on the ground, and peered onto the screen, glaring out at me in the darkness of the guardroom.

"Looks like …" Scott said, "… okay, got it." The screen flashed, and then a very small depiction of the guardroom appeared on screen. He thumbed a button to fast forward it, and we stood there watching guards flow in and out of the room, unconcerned, unharried, like they were going about their daily business. "Whoa."

Scott paused the image, a perfect freeze frame. I stared at it as he thumbed it back a few seconds and everything changed. The tape began to play normally, and two guards were standing in the middle of the room, talking, one of them with a cup of coffee in his hand.

A few seconds passed, and suddenly they both dropped without warning or notice, with only a flash of black in the image to herald anything changing. Blood spurted from their backs and they writhed in pain as they fell, curling into the fetal position.

"Go back," I said. "Can you freeze the video and walk it forward frame by frame?"

"I think so," Scott said, his tongue out of his mouth in concentration. He rewound it to a point when both guards were still standing and then paused it. The images resumed but more slowly, like someone was showing us a series of still images, a stop-motion video starring the guards whose faces we couldn't even see.

"There it is," Zollers said calmly, as Scott stopped the forward progress of the recording.

A figure in black was standing behind one of the guards, a figure that had not been there just one frame—one second—earlier. A knife the size of my forearm was clutched in his hand, and his dark hair looked like it was hanging in tangles. Even through the grainy footage and on the small screen, I knew him. I knew him and my heart thumped in fear because of it.

I let out a slow breath, a hiss of hatred. "Weissman."

Chapter 26

JAMES

The first breath of autumn had come to Minneapolis even though it was not nearly fall yet. James Fries felt it in the cool wind prickling his skin, and he cursed it. It rustled in the trees as he walked along the cool street, wishing that the sun overhead would do more to heat the day but knowing that it was a pointless hope.

It even smelled like fall, he conceded. The leaves on the trees were still green, so at least there was that, but September was nearly here and that was always the beginning of the end. He despised the winters here, despised being in Minnesota in general, but somehow he hadn't found the courage to leave. Why? He asked himself that on a daily basis. No answer was forthcoming.

He kept a steady pace as he walked along the tree-lined street, houses on both sides perched over him. He didn't know exactly why they built them this way, ten feet above the street with stone terraced steps that you had to climb to get up there. For the basements, he supposed. He'd been living in one of the older areas of Minneapolis for the last few months. He'd switched after the last time Sienna Nealon had found him. She'd shot him, for crying out loud. Twice.

That had been just before Omega went out of business. Scary times, knowing that the storm was blowing his way. He'd heard the whispers about Century, gotten a briefing or five with everything HQ had been willing to share at the time, but it'd had been months since London had gone dark.

Now all he had were rumors.

Even after all this time, James couldn't shake the idea that all of this—all the crap that had blown his way—had all started on the day he met Sienna Nealon. That smug, hard-edged little bitch. She was a frosty one. And damaged in all the wrong ways. Fries preferred his conquests with a little more innocence, a little more prettiness, and a lot more sweetness. That girl was as bitter as a hemlock milkshake.

He glanced over his shoulder involuntarily, and for the first time he took note of the two big guys behind him.

No, big wasn't an adequate descriptor. They were huge. He could see the long, red hair and beard of one of them. The other looked cleanly shaven. They were moving up on him fast, and Fries started to feel just a little bit nervous.

Was this how it was happening elsewhere? He didn't have any friends—incubi weren't beloved in the meta world, after all—but he'd read the Omega reports about metas disappearing elsewhere in the world. There were too many stories of it happening, too much evidence that the China and India explosions hadn't been accidents or regional disputes for him to dismiss it.

He took one look back at them, the two mountains of men, and he started to run.

The pre-fall air stung his cheeks. His breath exploded out of him. He didn't run. He didn't like to run. Fries didn't need to exercise; he maintained his physique just by being young and being a meta. What was the point of exercising when you were already a god?

Heavy footfalls behind him caused him to look back. The two men were pounding up the sidewalk toward him like he was walking. They ran with fury and speed, and Fries suddenly regretted not exercising.

They caught him after a block, one of them catching him by the collar and yanking him back. A leather-gloved hand descended over his mouth and strong arms gripped him tight enough to numb his forearm.

He felt a snap and his left arm broke with a screaming pain. A moment later his right followed, and he shouted his anguish into the leather glove but it did little good, making only a muffled sound.

An arm wrapped snug around his ribs and then broke three of them through the slow application of pressure. He screamed again, near soundlessly. It was like a high-pitched whistle in his own skull.

"If I squeeze him hard enough, do you think I can pop his head off?" a gravelly voice asked. He couldn't see, couldn't even judge where it came from, the pain was too overwhelming.

"Probably," came the answer from a voice just as gravelly. It almost sounded like the same person. Twins? he wondered. The gloved hand pushed in on his mouth and James felt his front teeth break loose of his gums. "Remember that guy in Switzerland that time?"

"Heh," came a guffaw. "That was fun."

"Still, maybe this time we should keep it neat. It is a city street in daylight, after all."

There was a snort. "You worried about the cops? I think we can take 'em. After all … it's been done before in this town."

"I wouldn't go basing my life's ambitions on what *he's* done."

"No," the reply came. James's head was swimming, and the pain was everywhere. "No, that's not a line I'd want to cross over, either. But still, he showed us it's possible."

"Let's wrap this up."

James felt himself spinning, a slow twirl. The hand stayed in his mouth all the while. He felt a few more teeth break free and realized that there were tears of pain on his cheeks, chilling in the air as he spun. He saw the face of the man who held him—

Oh, God, the face.

"I like to look my victims in the eyes as I kill them," the guy in front said. Red hair. All red. Like a lion's mane of red. No, not like a lion. Wrong animal. Like a—

There was a cracking, popping noise in James's head. He couldn't tell exactly where it came from. His chest? No … his neck. His throat. His head sagged, limp, held up by the hand that was closed up around his face. His jaw broke, and that one was louder and more obvious. He felt pressure on his lower face.

"That's a new one," the clean-shaven one said from behind the red-haired monster. "Might make him tougher to identify without dental records."

"Who cares?" Red asked. His eyes were like black pools of darkness. Like looking into the sun during an eclipse.

"Not me," the man behind Red said. "Hurry up and finish."

There was a last snapping, and a flash, and Fries felt the feeling disappear from his fingers, toes, and everywhere else. Red's eyes were the last thing he saw, and he wondered—thinking of all the women he'd killed—if they'd felt like this when he'd looked into their eyes? Looked into their eyes and—

Chapter 27

SIENNA

I was sitting on a plane on the runway at Phoenix's Sky Harbor International Airport, letting the blower above me churn barely warm air into my face. I hated the smell of planes, that filtered, sterile air. It reminded me of the medical unit at the old Directorate, where I'd spent more than my fair share of time in a bed, recovering from some grievous wounding or another.

I was feeling squeezed, with Zollers on the aisle side and Scott on the window side, looking out. He was still sullen, and hadn't said more than a few words since we'd left the wreckage of the prison. The local PD was on the scene along with the FBI, which was managing the fallout for us thanks to Foreman's intervention. Better them than me.

I had an inkling that Foreman was going to take some heat over this, but it wasn't like there was anything I could do about it. With the local PD on the scene, news was bound to leak unless someone spun it as a research facility or something. I didn't know how it was going to wash out, but I was glad to be well clear of the mess.

Zollers was trying to be considerate, tucking his elbow in so I could have the armrest. Scott was not conscious enough of those of us around him to do anything of the sort, and so I had his elbow almost poking me in the ribs. "Why did I get stuck in the middle?" I mumbled, low enough that no human would have been able to hear me.

But my traveling companions were not humans. "Because you're just too nice," Zollers said.

I felt a frown come on. "I thought you were a mind reader, but it's like you don't know me at all."

He let out a soft chuckle at that and turned back to reading his magazine. I knew we'd have to call a meeting as soon as we were back on campus; there were things that had to be dealt with, and we needed to get everyone on the same page. I hated meetings, but we needed a plan. We needed a strategy. We'd dealt Century some unexpected damage from our expedition to Vegas, and they'd struck back. I doubted that it'd be the last bit of striking back Weissman would do, so we needed to figure something out soon.

I turned to look at Scott. He'd been my faithful right hand in Vegas. He had come with me to cheer me up, and he had. I was scared but felt myself returning to forward motion again, no longer frozen and paralyzed by this sense of inevitability that I'd had after my encounter with Sovereign. We'd struck a blow against this terrible destiny that he was trying to impose on us as if by divine fiat, and it gave me confidence we could do more.

Scott, on the other hand, seemed completely demoralized. Zollers's words about losses to my team hitting harder than losses to Century rang in my ears. I couldn't afford to have Scott out of action right now, wandering in the desert. For more reasons than one.

"Scott," I said gently, and he looked as if he were awakening. He turned his head to me, eyes bleary and red. I thought it was from lack of sleep, but there was no guarantee it was. Scott was sensitive; I had nearly forgotten that his breakup with Kat had put him hard on the bench only a few months earlier.

"What?" he asked.

I tried to figure out how to approach what needed to be said without driving him deeper into his shell. "I'm sorry."

He blinked, red eyes looking at me in confusion for a second before I saw them get jaded. "Are you really sorry for what we did? Or are you sorry that I'm feeling the way I am about it?"

I paused as I thought about lying. "I'm sorry you feel the way you do about it," I finally said, hoping the truth would set me free but doubting it all the way.

His entire face reddened. "Sienna, what we did was wrong."

I stared back at him, trying to keep myself expressionless. "In a perfect world, maybe."

"In a perfect world?" He nearly exploded, but controlled himself just in time, lowering his voice back to a whisper. "Sienna, we—" He paused, face twitching with emotion. "How does this make us any better than them?"

I surveyed him, watched him watching me, waiting for an answer. "I'm not worried about being better than them. I'm worried about helping you all survive them. You can live the rest of your life trying to be a superior being after the threat of them murdering you isn't hanging over every day of it."

"It's just so wrong," he said, shaking his head.

"This is war," I said. "Every place we tread is a battlefield, and the people we are up against are not going to politely declare that they're going to kill us before they try. They're hiding in plain sight, they're sneaky and they're vile, and they will not hesitate to wipe us out however they can. We are outnumbered, outgunned, and if we fight this war the moral way—the way that would allow your conscience to sleep easily at night, every one of you will die. Maybe you're okay with martyring yourself on the altar of whatever morality you feel you're upholding by following the good and lawful way you'd like to conduct this fight," I leaned closer to him, so my nose was almost touching him, "but I don't want to look back in a hundred years as the only survivor and have my regret be that I wish I'd fought harder to save our people."

He looked at me with dull eyes. "Are you really fighting to save our people? Or are you fighting because you're afraid you'll be looking back in a hundred years as the prisoner of Sovereign?"

I didn't flinch, though I felt it inside. Hot anger bubbled in me as I heard the engines start. "I'm fighting because while you'll all die if Sovereign wins, I'll lose my life. Yes, I have a personal stake in this. So do you. So does every meta. If you think my lot will be better than yours if we fail, I'm more than willing to exchange places with you. You can go be Sovereign's bride and I'll die in your stead, how about that?" On that one he flinched.

"I spent twelve years locked away in my house," I said. "Then I spent a year with the Directorate doing their bidding, putting off nearly everything I wanted to do and I've spent the last six months running my ass off trying to figure out how to save what's left of the metahuman race." My fingers came up and massaged my face. "We spent the last two days in Vegas identifying corpses, fighting enemies and chasing leads. I didn't gamble a dollar and I didn't have so much as a drop to drink. I'm tired, Scott. It feels like I've been in a cage my whole life, watching and hearing about everyone else living but me. I want to live, Scott. I want to live my life instead of having my life—and my job—run me, own me and break me."

I sat back in my seat. Scott stared at me for another moment, then turned back to the window. I glanced out to see bright sunshine lighting the runway as we taxied.

I leaned my head back and felt myself lull. I'd meant every word. Except for my time with Zack, I'd done nothing but that which was expected of me since I was a child. I'd been punished, forced, guided and tormented. I'd watched my only boyfriend die in a betrayal that still sickened me to think of it.

The sunlight flared outside as the plane turned, casting a long band of light on me. I wanted to live. I wanted to see the world without the fear of Century and Sovereign hanging over my head. I wanted to be free.

I felt the plane leave the ground, weightless, fighting against the gravity bringing it down, and I wondered if I'd ever be able to achieve that for myself. Then I remembered all the baggage I carried, waiting for me somewhere below, and a dark pit settled in my stomach. My destiny was going to be something else entirely, I suspected.

Chapter 28

The Agency had a different smell to it, I thought as I made my way into my office. It was fresher somehow, like someone had come in and cleaned while I was gone. I set my bag behind my desk. It didn't seem quite as heavy as when I'd left.

There were memos sitting in a tray on the corner of my desk. I suspected they were mostly recycling bin fodder, things that concerned Ariadne more than me, but ended up being CC'd my way for review. I tried to read them all, but unless they had an operational component, I usually filed them in the circular bin as quickly as I could rule out their importance.

I hadn't been in my office for more than ten minutes when I heard a knock at the door. It was the kind of quiet rap that I might have missed if I'd been immersed in something important. I was reading a document on the background of our financials involving trading activity on the New York Stock Exchange over the last sixty days though, and it was heading to the recycling bin shortly, so I heard the knock. "Come in," I said.

After a moment's pause, the door cracked open. Karthik's dark face peeked in through the inch-wide gap between door and frame, and I smiled. "Do you have a moment?" he asked, always impeccably polite.

"Come on in," I said, tossing the paper I was reading into the recycling bin. "You just spared me at least sixty seconds more of misery attempting to read this memo, so I figure I've got at least that much to give to you instead."

"Ah," Karthik said, dead serious, "I will endeavor to keep it brief, then."

"Karthik," I said, and he looked up, "I was kidding about the time limit. What's up?"

He hesitated, his whole body telling me that he didn't want to speak his mind. "You look … different … than when you left."

"I feel … different," I said. "More purposeful. Like we accomplished something while we were away. I don't know if you heard—"

"I heard," Karthik said, his head bowed. He wouldn't even look at me. "You did well. Thirteen more removed from the equation." He glanced up, just for a second. "Which makes what I am about to say all the harder."

I peered at him and felt myself leaning forward involuntarily. "What is it?"

"We are leaving," he said, and it rushed out like air surging from a hole in a tire. "The other British metas and I. There was a discussion … and I unfortunately came in on the losing side of it."

"Leaving?" I asked, feeling the numb shock spreading through me. "Leaving for … where?"

"Back to London," he said, and I could tell even through my surprise that he was crestfallen. "They voted to run … and I feel I owe it to them to protect them."

"But London …" My back hit the chair as I felt my weight shift. "No offense, Karthik, but you can't protect them. Not against Century."

"Neither can you," he said, but he didn't say it in an accusatory way, "and they know that."

"But I'm trying—"

"Your absence in Vegas following the death of Breandan and the others," Karthik said, almost mournfully, "along with the sudden shuffle back and forth on the night Sovereign came here … it's left them with a lack of confidence in their safety."

"And they'll be safe in London?" I asked, feeling as angry as if he'd insulted me. "With only you to protect them?"

His lips were a thin line, his eyes turned down. "I believe the argument that won the case was that you are the biggest target in this war at present, the most likely to get hit. They have seen what even a minimal response from Century brings, in the form of death to some of our most dear. While you have been leading, these people have been followers, watching from the distant back of the queue. They don't see what you do, and they don't hear my arguments in your favor. They hear that you killed thirteen of Century's assassins and they fear what reprisal will fall upon them for it. Last time it was only ten, after all, and it landed upon some of ours."

"I can't …" I struggled for words. "I don't see how they'll be any safer in London."

"It is possible they will not be," Karthik said. "And I have argued this; but mine was the only vote against leaving."

I felt a cold anger settle in on me. "Do they know they're going to die?"

Karthik didn't rise to my goad; instead the sadness seemed to settle in on him like a cloak weighing him down. "I think they know it's coming and are scared enough to try and delay it as long as possible."

My anger broke like it was a stick I'd been waving. Karthik had grabbed it from my hand and snapped it over his knee with his honesty. "Okay," I said, feeling nothing but loss and resignation. "We'll get them a plane."

Karthik's eyes came up. "I am sorry. I wish I could stay, but—"

"You want to protect your countrymen," I said, and my mouth was dry again. Why did this always happen in my times of greatest stress? "Karthik, you—"

"I doubt I will be of much help to you," he said, head still bowed. "And I have committed to help these people. I committed to it before we ever voted to follow you over here. I need to live up to my commitment now."

"Would it help if I told you how much we needed you?" I stood.

"Would it help if I told you what a grand and glorious fight it's going to have to be for us to win? If I told you how long the odds are, how stacked they are against us—"

"You could deliver your own version of the St. Crispin's Day speech if you so desired," Karthik said, and I could see the hurt in his eyes. "And I would indeed hold myself cheap if you come out of this, defeating Century against all these odds without my help."

I tried to decide what to say to that. I could almost feel the guilt radiating off of him. I needed his help; I needed everyone's help, didn't I? It felt that way, like every person I had on my side was another bullet in the gun. I was going to run out of shots before I ran out of targets. "You should honor your commitment to your countrymen, then," I said, and tried to be sincere about it. "You should keep your word."

He glanced up at me, and I saw his expression waver. "I will …" Words failed him, and he stayed silence for almost a full minute. "I will see them safely home and protect them for as long as I can." He made a slight bow to me. "I wish you all the fortune in this desperate fight." Without waiting for a reply, he turned and slipped back out through the door. I wondered if it was because he was as overrun with emotion as I was.

"We'll need it," I said after he'd left. "We'll need all the luck … and all the help we can get." And my thoughts fixed again on a place where more help waited, deep inside me, and wondered what I would have to do in order to get them to agree to render it.

Chapter 29

I knelt again in the forest floor outside the Agency. I caught myself still thinking of it as the Directorate, even though it hadn't been that for months. I wondered if I'd ever think of it as the Agency, or ever really consciously think of it as a place I helped run rather than being a place where I had grown up in so many ways.

The midday sun was shedding its light overhead. I was sweating under my suit jacket. I'd kept it on because I had a meeting in an hour or so, but I wanted to try this again first. I closed my eyes and ignored the bright sun shining through my eyelids. I tried not to notice the scent of the pine needles that were clinging to the knees of my pants, but they were pungent. Far more so than a car air freshener.

In a moment I was transported into the darkness in my head. My own personal Stonehenge of metal boxes surrounded me, looming ominously in the darkness. I didn't move this time, just stood there and unlocked every single one of them with my mind. I opened the doors, and they squealed their hinges. I looked at each of them in turn, staring into the darkness.

"Hey," Zack said, but it was terse. I felt a pinch of guilt.

"Hey," I replied. I hoped I wasn't going to have to deal with him being in an uproar with the rest of them. I watched the entry to each of the boxes; not one of my meta prisoners was coming out voluntarily, it appeared.

"So …" he said, and I could hear the accusation as he spoke. "Scott?"

"Oh, God, not now," I muttered. "I hate to be insensitive, but you're kind of dead. Please don't be a jealous ex."

He gave me a scathing look. "I may be dead, but I still have to watch everything you do for as long as you live, apparently, so forgive me for being a little touchy about the fact that you're taking up with one of my friends only six months after I died."

"I haven't 'taken up with him,'" I said, just a little defensively. "And in case you haven't noticed, it turns out just being my cold-hearted self is enough to scare him away, so I wouldn't worry too much."

"The Little Doll is quite the frost princess," Wolfe said from the darkness behind me. I turned to find him out of his box, still clutching at the edges. "She drives away and destroys everyone around her, given enough time."

I stared back at him warily. "What about you, Wolfe? Have I driven you away?"

His eyes flickered. "The Little Doll destroyed the Wolfe."

"You're still standing there," I said. "So you're not totally destroyed."

"But the Wolfe is incorporeal," Wolfe said, and he threaded his way toward me in a slow walk, like a predator stalking. "Unable to affect the world. Unable to touch, to feel, to taste—"

"I sympathize," I said, in a voice that probably didn't convey much sympathy. I couldn't find it in myself to be sorry he wasn't able to slaughter people anymore. "Being somewhat unable to touch myself," I amended.

"But the Little Doll can touch the world, oh yes," Wolfe said, eyes narrowed. "The Little Doll holds the whole world in her hands, oh yes, she does. If she falls, and it tips out of her hands, it crashes to the ground and breaks. The Little Doll may not be able to touch a person without hurting and destroying, but she touches the world in ways no one sees."

I tried to gauge his emotion. Why was he telling me this? "Does that displease you, Wolfe?"

He took a long, seething breath. "The Wolfe cares not one way or the other. The Wolfe sees things the Little Doll doesn't, though. Sees the works of her foes and knows their names. The Little Doll is in far, far over her head."

I looked at him coldly. I couldn't help it. "I live over my head. Every day."

He wasn't leering, not exactly. There was an aloofness in what he was saying that was unusual even for Wolfe. His joyful smugness was gone. "The problem with being in over her head for too long is that eventually the Little Doll will have to take a breath or else she'll drown." He circled closer to me. "And the Little Doll can feel the water, can't she? Pressing in on all sides? Can the Little Doll feel the pressure? Feel the primal urge?"

I didn't blink, but his words were like claws to my heart, triggering some emotion and hurt within. "Yes," I whispered. "Yes, I feel it. I feel it every day. Like I'm drowning and all I can do is keep thrashing."

"The Little Doll's thrashing has done some good," Wolfe said. "She's fighting hard for her life. But blindly."

His black eyes circled closer to me. He was all shadow now, even though he was close. All the light had fled from this place, like it had been drained out by the slow onset of despair that was infecting me. "Help me," I said, and it came out choked, like a plea. I stared at each of the steel monuments around me. "Please. Help me. I need … help."

One of the doors slammed, then another, then another. "Ahhh," Wolfe said, and now there was glee in his voice. "Desperation. Begging. Fear. Does the Doll see the future coming? Can she taste the despair as the hour approaches?"

"Yes," I said, and I shook as I said it. "I can feel it. One moment I'm hopeful, like there's a chance to batter our way through, and the next I remember that there are eighty of them and maybe eight of us. It hangs on me like a cloud, surrounds me like I'm drowning in it." I took a step closer to Wolfe and looked into the black eyes.

"Help me. Please."

Another door slammed behind me, and Wolfe stared back at me. "Oh, Little Doll …" His face broke into a wide smile. "Little Doll, begging for help, asking for the Wolfe to save her from drowning. Take a deep breath, Little Doll." His face receded into the shadows. "… and drown."

Dark laughter filled the space around me, a cackling from Wolfe that was as hideous as any I'd ever heard. It was hearty, filled with joy, and I slammed him back into his box and locked the door with only a thought.

I broke my trance and I was back on the floor of the forest, kneeling as the sun sunk low in the sky. My breathing was rushed, coming in gasps as though I hadn't taken a breath the whole time I was in the dark. The sound of laughter hung in my ears, echoing; the last ringing taunt of the cruelest creature I'd ever known.

Chapter 30

"So you let them leave?" Reed sounded incredulous, voice wafting through the air like the scent of the coffee someone had brought into the conference room and left on a side table. It was nearing sundown now, but I still had a strong cup in front of me steaming over the top of the white Styrofoam that enclosed it. "Are you kidding me?"

"I wish," Ariadne said from her place down the table. "I arranged the transport myself."

"Wow," Kat said from her place next to Janus down the table to my right, "that uhm … doesn't really seem like the smartest move. You know, strategically speaking." She tilted her head and flipped her blond hair off her skinny neck, wide eyes still staring at me.

"This is a volunteer army," I said, trying to gauge the mood at the table. Scott was still sullen, down a little ways to the left. Reed was sitting at the opposite end next to my mother, who was watching me wordlessly, face a mask. "I can't force people to fight."

"But could your new telepath friend?" Agent Li was sitting about midway down the left side of the conference table, and he had been watching Dr. Zollers suspiciously since Zollers had entered the room. I wondered if Zollers was insulted by it, but then I remembered he could read Li's mind and probably realized that he wasn't being singled out for this treatment; Li was suspicious of everyone.

"It's possible," Zollers said mildly, "but I don't think Sienna wanted to cross that particular line."

"Oh, so we finally found one she won't cross," Scott said. "Good to know."

Reed frowned at him. "What's that all about?"

"He's angry because we burst into the Century safe house in Vegas with guns-a-blazing," I said. "He doesn't feel it was a 'fair' fight."

"All's fair in love and war," Reed said with a shrug.

"But presumably you wouldn't use a shotgun in your love life," Kat said, her pretty face crimped in concentration. "Although if you did, it would explain why you don't have a girlfriend."

"I don't have a girlfriend because we're at the end of days for our people," Reed said at something slightly less than a growl, "and for some reason I'm overly focused on the imminent danger to our lives rather than the somewhat less pressing need to get laid."

There was a stark silence at the table until my mother spoke up. "Good priorities," she said, all business. "Now, perhaps we could talk more about this war we're fighting and focus less on the inferred sex lives of our elderly members?" She cast an uncomfortable look toward Janus and Kat, who blushed.

"What is our next move?" Janus asked, and I could hear his discomfort. He turned toward me. He still looked awfully weathered, as though his time in a coma had not been at all restful.

"Offense," I said. "We need to attack and keep attacking. A counter-blow is eventually coming, and we need to stay tight and sweep as many of their pawns off the table as we can before it connects."

"What about our pawns?" Li asked, and I wondered if he was doing it just to be aggravating. "Doesn't the thought of losing them concern you?"

"If we turtle up and try to play defense again like we did before," I said, "we will lose. They will come for us, they will overwhelm us, and they will probably kill all of you. If we can strike them and take as many of them as possible piecemeal before that happens, we might—maybe—be able to even the odds enough to win the final fight."

"Wow, that was stirring," Reed said into the shocked silence that followed my pronouncement. "Such confidence."

"Would you like me to lie to you?" I didn't snap at him, just laid it out there without a lot of care. "By my count there are six metas at this table in the fight and a little over eighty of them remaining on Century's team."

"Seven," Janus said quietly. "I think you have forgotten to count yourself."

"What?" I looked around. "Sorry. Seven. You're right, I forgot myself. Foreman makes eight, if he's available." I leaned forward. "And if anyone wants to take themselves out of that number, now would be the time to do it, because I need everyone to be all-in from here on out."

"Where's the line, Sienna?" Scott turned his chair to face me, looking down the black-glass table. "What won't we do to stop Century?"

"There's nothing I won't do to stop Century." I felt my jaw harden in resolve as I spoke.

"Would you kill civilians?" Scott asked.

I hesitated. "No. I mean, why would I have to—"

"Because they'll use them as shields," Scott said, dark clouds brewing over his face. "If they know that's your line, don't you think they'll find a way to start hiding behind people? Take hostages for their safe houses; start executing them when you break down a door? I mean, they basically had Zollers like that, they just failed to finish him. Are you willing to kill innocent people to win this fight?"

I froze. I hadn't even considered that.

"You're damned right," my mother said from the opposite end of the table. "Do you know what those peoples' lives will be worth if Century wins? Not a damned thing."

Scott wheeled to face her. "So you think Century's plan is to wipe out every person on the face of the earth?"

"I don't know what Century's plan is," my mother said, and I could see the tautness in the way she answered. If this had been our house, and Scott had been me, he'd be heading toward the box right now. "But I know it involves conquest and control, which means anyone who survives is going to be stooping and bowing to Sovereign's new world order." She folded her arms in front of her. "Better to be dead now than a servant in whatever 'paradise' he's got planned."

"That's not your choice to make," Ariadne said, flushed. "Some people would rather live—"

"Like slaves?" My mother cut her off. "Peasants in the service of a dictator?"

"Yes," Janus said slowly. "Some would willingly choose to live for nothing in a horrible half-life where the boot of Century rests forever on the back of their neck rather than risk dying in an effort to throw that boot off. I have seen it, time and again, over the years of my life."

"Well, before we all go crying, 'FREEDOM!' and tossing our big swords through the air," Reed said dryly, "maybe we could focus on the here and now, where Century hasn't yet decided to start holding people hostage."

"Don't you get it?" Scott said, turning his dull eyes to Reed. "We're already wandering out past the lines we would have drawn a year ago when we were fighting Omega. I want to know how far she's going to go to win this war. Where is the new line? What's the limit for what she's willing to do to beat Sovereign and Century?"

"It sounds to me like you're asking at what point we surrender," my mother said coldly, "and my answer to that is that we ought to fight to the last breath, because you're going to be dead anyway ten seconds after you offer your surrender to Century. They will kill us all." She looked down the table. "Human and meta alike."

"You don't know that," Scott said, a little louder.

"If you are a metahuman, I would say the evidence is fairly compelling," Janus said.

"But the humans," Scott said. "We don't know what they mean to do. We don't know what's going to happen." He looked me full in the eyes. "I hope you know I'm not a coward. I want to live, but I'm not afraid to die in the course of this. But what we're doing is …" He swallowed hard. "Sienna, what we're doing is horrible. We walked into that house and took lives like it was the most inconsequential thing in the world. Like we were swatting flies, or stomping on ants." He leaned over the table, and I could see his heart break as he spoke. "You were so … cold about it … like it was just nothing—"

"Scott," I said, cutting him off. "Later." I looked around the table, and saw the truth in the eyes of almost everyone else. My mom got it; she was looking away. Janus got it; his head was lowered. Reed was the opposite, but I could see he'd caught it, too. His head was leaned back and he was staring at the ceiling. Zollers knew; of course he did. He'd read it in Scott's mind from the beginning, and part of me cursed him for not telling me. He cast me a sympathetic look from down the table.

Scott just sat there, mouth slightly open, like he wanted to say something else. I hoped he wouldn't, though, not now. We had a war to plan, after all, and this was a distraction that needed to be dealt with in private. And it would be, right after the meeting. I just hoped it wasn't too late.

Because Scott had finally seen what everyone else already knew, and I'd been too dumb to realize it. Scott had finally opened his eyes—his naïve, half-lidded eyes—and seen the real Sienna Nealon, the one who had been brought back into the world after that cold, autumn night when the Directorate exploded around her and her boss had forced her to kill her own boyfriend.

Now he was finally seeing it, seeing the darkness within me. The hard, razor-edged me who had been there all along … and it had scared him so badly I might lose him forever.

Chapter 31

After the meeting, I'd only had about five seconds with Scott before the interruption had come. It was just enough time to look him in the eye, open my mouth and start to say something before the knock had come at my door. I was standing inches away from him next to my desk, close enough to hear his every breath, close enough to catch the faint whiff of his manly cologne. I caught the hurt in his eyes as I grimaced and said, "Yes?"

The door cracked open and Ariadne poked her head in. "Problem."

"Don't talk to me about problems," I said, looking around Scott at her, "talk to me about solutions."

She cocked her head and gave me the annoyed look I had always associated with mothers for some reason. I caught it from Ariadne more of the time than even from my own mother, who tended more toward spitting rage than plain annoyance. "We got a report of a dead body in Minneapolis."

I felt my facial muscles tighten. "I, uh … I don't want to be unfeeling as I say this, but I believe that's a somewhat common occurrence in Minneapolis."

"Killed in broad daylight," Ariadne brandished a piece of paper. "Witnesses report that a large man with red hair held the victim up in the air as he crumpled his lower head like he was squeezing a pop can."

I stared at her. "Okay, so, maybe not so common." I shot a look of apology at Scott, whose expression was already shrouded, like he was hiding what he felt—but poorly. "We should—"

"Go check it out, yeah," Scott said, and the sullenness came out. "Always the mission."

I wanted to slap him across the face and remind him that failure of the mission meant his death, at which point we'd never have a chance to explore his fragile emotions, but I decided that wouldn't produce the right results. So I shut up. "We can talk on the way, if you'd like—"

"Go on without me," he said, shaking his head. "Maybe we'll talk when you get back."

I shot a pleading look at Ariadne, but she just shrugged, and I turned my focus back to Scott, who was now stone-faced. "Go on. You've got important things to do."

"Yes," I said, "and pulling you back in the boat is right at the top of my list."

"I'm not out of your boat quite yet," he said, "but you might consider taking a break from rowing when you get back if you want me to keep from falling out."

I felt a pained expression paralyze my face. Did he really not see what was at stake? Was it not obvious that this was what NEEDED to be done? "We'll talk when I get back," I said, and let my fingers brush his face. I cringed as I passed, realizing that I'd just used up three or four seconds of my allotted time to touch him for the day, and I might need them later to help soothe him.

I passed Ariadne as she held the door open for me and almost ran into Reed, who was standing just behind her. "Why are you lurking?" I asked him as the three of us awkwardly tried to clear out of my doorway. The noise of the cubicle farm behind him carried over a pleasant hum of activity, even at this late hour of the day.

"I was over there talking to one of the analysts and I heard Ariadne's news," Reed said with a tight smile. "Figured I'd go with you to Minneapolis."

"Lovely," I said, "you can drive." I started past him.

"What is it with you and driving?" he asked as he fell in behind me on the way to the elevators.

"I don't feel comfortable doing it," I said as I pressed the call button. The sharp ding of the elevator arrival tone followed a half-second later. "I mean, I've only been driving for a year and a half or so. I've taken the courses, and I *can* do it, I'd just rather someone else do it."

"Well, okay, Miss Daisy," he said as the elevator doors slid closed with a low thumping noise. The elevator box smelled stuffy, nothing like the brisk fall air I'd gotten a taste of outside. "I can drive."

I looked over at him. "You're not going to give me crap about playing rough with Century, are you? Because if so, I can drive myself—"

He held up a hand to stay me. "I'm not super enthused about what you're doing, but it's dire times. I think Scott's problem is that he's shaken because he hasn't killed many people and—I mean, he's not really over the first kill thing yet, and now you've got him taking a shotgun to unarmed people." He shrugged. "It's messy. I remember my first kill rattling me. Didn't yours give you the guilt for a while?"

"Kinda sorta not really," I said. "But my first kill was Wolfe, so …"

The elevators dinged open in the lobby and I started to get out, but found someone blocking the path. "Janus," I said with a nod, and tried to pass him. He shifted to block my path, and it took me only a second to realize he was doing it intentionally. "Let me guess—we need to talk."

"It is almost as though you are reading my mind," Janus said with a faint smile that didn't crinkle the crow's feet at his eyes. "You are going out?"

"Checking out a body in Minneapolis," I said as we crossed the lobby and passed through the security checkpoint. "Reports indicate it could be a meta attack."

"Lovely," he said, his tone suggesting it was anything but. "I will accompany you."

"This isn't about your former Omega recruits that just bailed on us, is it?" I asked, sending him a look laden with reproach.

"What? No," he said with a shake of the head as we cleared the front doors and the fall breeze whipped around us, rattling the heavy door. "They have made their choices, and while I regret that Karthik failed to realize that he would better serve the greater good by remaining here with us, I think having them gone will free you to focus on the important business of waging an offensive war, as you have stated is your intention. Keeping them here, worrying about defending them, it was all a distraction."

I paused in the front driveway loop. There was a Towncar sitting there, waiting suspiciously. I peered into the window and saw a set of keys in the ignition. "Is this ours?"

"It's the Agency's, yeah," Reed said. "Looks like a couple agents left it here."

"Take down the tag number and remind me to have security drag them over the coals later," I said, frowning as I opened the passenger door. "This is a case of grand theft auto waiting to happen."

"It's a closed campus," Reed said with amusement as he popped around and got in the driver's seat. "The only people who could steal it would have to be our employees, and they'd do it right under the nose of security with about a billion cameras to record them doing it. He turned the key in the ignition and I had a brief flash of paranoia, worrying that someone might have left a car bomb for me … just outside my workplace … on the off chance I might decide to commandeer that particular car…

Paranoia. Apparently, it's not just for my mother anymore.

"Can we talk?" Janus said from the back seat.

"Sorry," I said. "Go on." The smell of the leather interior was heavy, and I cracked the window to let the fall air creep into the car.

"You cannot let yourself be swayed by anyone who tells you that your tactics are unnecessary," Janus said. "This is a fight to the death, and Century has clearly proven whose death they would prefer it to be. Losing your nerve at this point would be a grave mistake."

"As in, it would lead to the graves of all of you," I said. "I agree, which is why I made my position plain in the meeting."

"I heard it," Janus said, "but I could sense your emotional surety begin to falter when Mr. Byerly posited a scenario in which innocent civilians might be harmed."

"My surety might falter when innocent civilians enter the picture," I said coolly as Reed steered the car out the front gate of the campus with a wave at the guardhouse, "but since they've yet to use human shields, I think we're safe from debate on this point for a while longer. Also," I said, mildly annoyed, "all you people digging in my head? Does that ever stop being annoying? Because I'm thinking you had to have had complaints from the HR department at Omega for this—"

"We are speaking of inconsequential and distracting matters again," Janus said with a wave of his hand. "And of course I had no complaints from the Human Resources department at Omega. I am an empath, I steer the course of people's emotions; do you think for a moment I would allow someone the luxury of having sufficiently ill feelings toward me that they would feel pressed enough to file a complaint?"

I exchanged a look with Reed, one of reluctant amusement. "You old dog, you," Reed said with a smile that was probably just this side of irritated. "Omega was the perfect environment for that type of corruption, wasn't it?"

"Old news," Janus said with a sigh. "They are dead, we are not. This war, though, it could well kill us all, and I would not care to be undone simply because you have failed to consider the options available to your enemy at the outset and plan your responses accordingly. Sovereign is a mind-reader; others in his group are as well—"

"Claire," I said tightly, remembering the stocky woman whose leg I had broken in Vegas.

"There will undoubtedly come a moment when they choose to throw your fears in your face," Janus said, all seriousness, "because that is what they do. They will find your weaknesses and strike at them. They will determine the stress and fracture points of your organization and press as hard as they can on them. They will break your support if they can, and you need to be prepared for that."

"I like that you think they won't just come in with overwhelming force and kill us," Reed said, not taking his eyes off the road. "You're more optimistic than I am."

"Why use a nuclear warhead to kill a cockroach?" Janus said with another sigh. "When a simple shoe will do the job?"

"Actually, from what I've heard, the boot is more likely to kill the cockroach than the nuke," Reed said.

"Because you think a cockroach can survive being heated to ten thousand degrees Fahrenheit?" Janus snapped. "Don't be ridiculous. Consider the logistics of hitting you with overwhelming force. Weissman is no fool—he has a plan, and will use whatever it takes to get the job done and no more. He has his teams scattered, doing what they must to wipe out our people. Only if he fails at his first attempt to destroy you will he summon those carefully laid tendrils back to himself for use in finishing the task, because to do any more would delay the implementation of his efforts."

I had to grudgingly concede that point. "And if there's anything Weaselman has shown us thus far, it's that he's trying to keep to some sort of timetable, or else he would have come at us with something stronger than a mercenary unit last time."

"Yes, he is conserving his resources to keep his plan on

schedule," Janus said urgently. He was leaning forward, speaking almost directly into my ear. He was kind of loud, actually.

"Which works in our favor," Reed said.

"Indeed," Janus said, "but it is a double-edged sword. One or two more hard hits to Century and he will likely call in … the rest of his merry band, I think you would say?"

"Not sure that's how I'd put it," I said, "but I get your point. That could actually work in our favor, though. Getting all of Century together in one place …"

"You would never survive it," Janus said, shaking his head so obviously I could hear it move. "Do not even dwell on the insanity of trying to face such a cataclysm. Best we continue to take them bit by bit, as quickly as possible. I believe the most fitting word is … blitzkrieg."

"Because that doesn't have any historical associations we'd care to shed," Reed said with dark lines of a frown etched all over his face.

"Outside of the obvious—and distasteful—associations, the underlying principle is sound. We strike at them quickly, lightning-fast, hitting them in safe house after safe house, city after city, without mercy or pause." Janus thumped a fist into his hand.

"And how do we find them to hit them in such a manner?" Reed said, voice dripping with sarcasm. "Because I'm sure they're posting signs on every corner that say 'Century safe house.'" He snorted.

"Ah, but they have as much as done that," Janus said with deep satisfaction, "albeit inadvertently. You see, you have to consider that they never planned for someone to come after them, and so they never worried about carefully covering their tracks."

I glanced at Reed and he looked at me. Green trees were whooshing by outside his window, and the faint rush of the wind outside my cracked window was like white background noise for me to think to. "What are you talking about?" Reed asked. "You know how to find them?"

"I believe I do," Janus said, "and if you'll forgive me, I've set your man—J.J., I believe his name is—to testing my theory."

"You're forgiven," I said, "especially as J.J. is most definitely not, 'my man.'" I shuddered then craned my head around to see Janus, who was sitting back in the seat now, with a look of deep satisfaction. "What did you do? How did you tell him to find them?"

"I'm curious about that myself," Reed said, almost dismissive. "Since we've been looking for hints to Century's location for the last year and haven't found squat."

"It's very simple once you know what to look for," Janus said. "And the reason you can't imagine it being so easy is because you—my young friend, you idealist, you—are a product of Alpha, that bastion of crusading do-gooders, out to destroy evil Omega." His voice carried great humor and an exaggerated emphasis on what he was saying that bordered on satire. "Whereas I am a product of Omega, where our focus was on … money." His eyes glittered behind his glasses. "So, you see, my boy, you would look for Century while thinking all the while, 'what would this evil group be doing?' I, on the other hand, know just as little of their motives as you…" his eyes twinkled, "but I know that if you want to catch them, you need to follow the money. And by revealing their safe house in Vegas, they have left a trail of money for you to follow … all the way back to wherever it originated from."

Chapter 32

I counted five cop cars on the scene as we pulled up. I was pretty well sick of the sight of cop cars by now, their flashing lights becoming a familiar code to me for nothing good. The street was nice and quiet, like a thousand others in the city. Naturally there were a few people standing outside watching, but that was nothing new.

I wished I'd brought a heavier coat when I started toward the knot of police cruisers surrounding the scene. All I had on was my suit jacket. I flipped open my FBI ID so the cop on the perimeter could see it and he nodded as I crossed under the police tape. The morgue wagon was parked nearby and there were no paramedics in sight, so I knew this one had been a lost cause from the get go.

The wind carried a hint of sulfur, blowing in off the factories just across the river. It wasn't strong, was actually barely noticeable, but to a meta, everything is far more obvious than it should be. I longed for a sip of coffee, but the sun was going down and I needed to sleep at some point.

I stopped just shy of the body that was covered in front of me and waited for one of the morgue guys to look up. When they didn't, I reached down and jerked the covering off the corpse. It was certainly a mess.

"With a face like that, I bet he didn't get many dates," Reed cracked. I gave him a sidelong glance and he quickly looked contrite. "Sorry."

"No, it's okay," I said, staring into the blank eyes of the corpse. They were already rolled up into the head. I stared at the cheekbones, tried to imagine the face when it was all put together normally. The jaw had been just crushed, like the guy became the

Muppet Beaker below his cheeks. Wrecked tissue and exposed bones were mashed up in the skin and blood. I couldn't recall seeing anything quite like this before, save for that time I'd beaten the head of Omega to death with a chair. Though that was slightly messier, I think. "He actually did get quite a few dates, just none that survived to go on a second."

"Huh, what?" Reed asked. I could see I'd lost him.

I felt a prickle of interest from Janus as he leaned forward to look at the corpse. "Fries," he said in surprise.

"Yep," I said. I'd recognize those eyes, that hair, those cheeks, anywhere. The clothing was spot-on, too, that preppy son of a bitch. "Looks like James came to the bad end I always predicted he would."

"Seriously?" Reed leaned over and squinted at the body. "That's James Fries?"

"Yeah," I said.

"Are you sure?" he asked.

I sent him a sidelong look that was full glare this time. "I'm sure. However long I live, I'm not likely to forget this loathsome shitbird." Or his lips, though those were now missing.

"Wow, Fries," Reed said. "What are the odds?"

"Very poor," Janus said, stiffly. "If you are suggesting this might be coincidence, I can tell you it is most certainly not."

"I'm starting to sense a pattern," I said, staring at the mangled corpse of James Fries, the only incubus I knew. "First Charlie, and now—"

"Yes," Janus said, nodding his head. "Century is killing all the incubi and succubi." He gave us a slow look, and I could see the weight of the news weighing on him. "Sovereign wants to make sure there is no one else with the power to oppose him."

Chapter 33

"This isn't the best news I've heard all week," my mother said sourly as I stared across my desk at her. "Is there anyone else even left?"

"You and me," I said, sliding a thin file across the desk. "All the other incubi and succubi we had on record are either dead or missing. I'm guessing dead. Weissman doesn't strike me as the type to leave a lot of loose ends."

"So am I next?" There was a joking quality to my mother's words, but I could feel the tension beneath them.

"Presumably," I said, with a little tension of my own.

She stared at me, and a softness came into her cold blue eyes. "I think there was a time you might have been gleeful in pronouncing that, so I guess I should take it as progress that you don't seem pleased."

"I'm not," I said, lowering my head. "I'm so not. Whatever there is between you and me," I said, waving a hand between us, "I'm mostly over it. I don't have time in my life to be bitter and angry at you anymore." I faked a smile. "Too many other people are vying for my bitterness and anger at present."

"You little liar." She rolled her eyes then turned serious. "I did it all for you, you know."

I stared back at her, keeping any hint of emotion off my face. "I believe you believe that."

She narrowed her eyes, and I wondered if she was going to split hairs with me over what I'd just said. She let it pass. "You know this Weissman better than I do; do you think he'll send these henchmen here to do the job?"

"I don't know what he's going to do," I said. "It's always a guessing game with these assholes."

"Are you done running?" she asked.

"I'm done running," I said. "I'll fight to the death now. Scorched earth all the way."

"That's grim," she said with a frown.

"Well, losing isn't exactly Plan A," I said. "But I'm all in. No matter what. Kill 'em all or die trying."

My mother hesitated, shuffling her feet and staring at them. I watched her, wondering what the hell had happened to the woman who used to casually lock me in an iron box when I defied her. Now she reminded me of the kid in our relationship, looking at her shoes and trying to figure out how to broach something with me. "Do you figure he'll punch out on you, now that we're getting so close to the end?"

I knew she was talking about Scott. "Maybe if he knew how close we were to the actual end, it wouldn't affect him so badly. But I think his heart's starting to catch up with his head." I lowered my voice. "You know I've murdered people. I'm not proud of it, but I've done it. Stuff so far over the line I can't even justify it. M-Squad. The Primus of Omega. Scott … he hasn't. I know it weighed on me. Still does. I just don't let it drag me all the way down by dwelling on it."

"Believe me, I know," she said. "You don't accumulate the record of wildfire captures that I did without putting a few in the ground along the way." She shuffled her feet again. "Along with a few innocents who were in the wrong place at the wrong time."

I felt my face freeze in a cringe. "How do you even deal with that? I mean, Rick from Omega, that was one thing; he was threatening me, trying to lord his power over me, and I think Wolfe just pulled my trigger at an opportune moment." I took in a sharp breath. "But a total innocent, caught in the crossfire?"

I didn't even want to fathom that. I flashed back to a moment a year and a half ago when I was chasing Henderschott, the armored ass, through Eden Prairie Center and he'd cast a clothing rack at a stroller. I'd pulled the baby out of the way and saved him. I tried to imagine what would have happened if I'd been a little too slow.

"This is war," my mother said. "It's unfortunate, but it happens. I was after this one wildfire who had done this spree of bank-robbing. He had hostages." She had a look that was as close to … haunted as I'd seen, save for the times she'd talked about Sovereign. "He'd already killed eighteen people by that point, was the focus of a three-state manhunt. He wanted to escape and he took hostages in hopes that we'd trade them to let him go. Killed one just to prove how serious he was."

"But you came at him anyway," I said, suspecting that I already knew the ending of this particular tale.

"He killed three before I got my hands on him." She kept her head bowed. "It was a tough decision, but I asked myself if he would do more damage if we let him get away than if I just ended him right then." She shrugged.

"That's cold math," I said. "Which I think is Scott's objection. He sees the people that get hurt, sees the damage through empathetic eyes. He still feels it. His soul isn't like mine, rubbed raw by all the terrible things I've done." I blinked and looked up at her. "I feel…numb to it. Like if I stop, the people I care about will die. So to me, these Century flunkies aren't even human." I pursed my lips. "I'm probably looking at it wrong. Less feeling. More…calculating."

"You have to be calculating," she said and leaned over my desk. Her dark hair fell around her face, and she wore a look of seriousness now, all mournful reminiscence gone. "You can't allow yourself the luxury of feeling it all now. The stakes are too high to go soft now. I know what other people would argue because I've heard it; your emotions, your better angels—that you should listen to them, mercy, peace, olive branch, all that crap." She stared down at me. "Do you think there's hope of mercy or peace from Sovereign and Weissman?"

"No," I said. "There will never be any mercy from Weissman. And Sovereign is just letting him do what he has to do, so long as he doesn't hurt me."

I caught the flicker behind her eyes. "So if he did hurt you—"

I sighed. "Don't even think it. You'd never pull it off, getting Sovereign to think Weissman had hurt me. He's a mind-reader."

"Yeah, I know," she said, sighing. "But you can't blame me; I'm just trying to show you how calculating you'll have to be to win this. You can either live in reality or run from it. It's your choice, but you can't get bitchy when it catches up to you and beats you to a bloody pulp. If you're going to win, you need to consider every option, every possibility, find every ally you can get your hands on. The stakes are too high and the odds are too long to leave any possibility unexamined, no matter how crazy or … unpleasant it might be to carry out."

I pondered that for a moment. "There is one possibility I hadn't considered. Not really that crazy, though it is a little unpleasant."

"Oh?" My mother arched an eyebrow at me. "What's that?"

"I think the time has come to meet one of my enemies face to face," I said, "and see if I can wring any truth out of him."

Chapter 34

"Scott," I said as I opened the door to my quarters. He was standing out in the hall in jeans and a t-shirt. I'd called for him a few minutes earlier and wondered if he'd even show.

"You had your message delivered by a runner," he said, holding up the little slip of paper in his hand. "We live just down the hall from each other; you could have just dropped by yourself." His cheeks were flushed, and I caught a whiff of alcohol.

Uh oh.

"I wanted you to be able to say no." I shut the door behind him. He led the way into the living room that was a step down from the entry and kitchen and stood there, just looking at my glass window. It was night, and the campus was lit, spread before us. It wasn't a terrible view, as far as things went, but it was no city skyline. "I didn't want to put you in an uncomfortable position of having to answer me face to face if you wanted to pass on talking."

"Ah," he said, still staring at the glass wall.

"Yeah." I stared at the back of his head. "Listen—"

"Let me just say it," he said, turning around. "I see their faces, Sienna. Burned into my memory." The mournful look, the quiver of his lip, they shut me right up. "When I shot at those mercs who invaded the dorms, it was unquestionably the right thing to do. Our metas were under attack, they killed some of our people …" He let his voice trail off for a moment. "When I took out those guys in the casino, that was pure, too. They came at me, they had ill intent, and when the dust settled, two of them were dead by my hand.

"But when I took a shotgun and kicked down the door of that

safe house …" His face hardened and I watched him shudder. "I see the first one when I close my eyes. I watch the look of surprise run over her face as I blasted it off with buckshot." His voice cracked. "I can see the red running in lines down the walls. And I didn't have a choice at that point, I had to keep going on to the next one, and the next one …"

"I'm sorry," I said, not sure what else to say.

"I don't want to be the weak link," Scott said, shaking his head. "I meant to stand by you to the end of this. I still mean to. What we're doing here … stopping Century … it's important work. But how we do it … feels like it should be more upright. More moral. This isn't even a grey area; we're deep in the black here."

"Lives are at stake," I said. "Do you not believe in the principle of self defense? Of being able to fight back when your life is on the line?"

"You know I do," Scott said. "I've proven I do. But this is not exactly self-defense. This is preemptive murder."

"They're coming, Scott," I said, urgently.

"I know!" He blurted it out, all fury. "I know they're coming. It's why I sent my parents to Canada, to get them out of the way! I know it's going to be bad, but … I just … I can't … I can't do it, Sienna. It's so …"

"It's not easy to live with," I said. "Your parents … they're the last family you have left?"

"You know it," he said, and I could see his face flush. "My aunt and uncle, the ones Wolfe killed? They were the only other immediate family we had. All the others were extended relations, like my … charming Aunt Judy. No one else we really knew."

"I'm glad your family is safe," I said, and took a step closer to him. "I just … I really need your help right now." I put a hand on his shoulder, brushed my fingernails against his cheek. "I've … come to rely on you. Not just because you're a strong meta, but … for other reasons." I bowed my head. "I don't want to lose you now."

"I'm not leaving you," Scott said, sighing. "I wouldn't do that. But … please … don't ask me to murder anyone. If they're coming at us, I will kill every one of them that comes, just … don't send me into a house with a shotgun and have me cut down unarmed people again. Please."

I could hear the note of pleading in his voice, the begging sound of a man who'd been broken by what he'd seen. What he'd done.

What I'd made him do.

The whole war so far flashed in front of my eyes. All the killing, all the deaths, and that same ratio that expressed one thing—the odds overwhelmingly against us. The bishops and rooks being gradually pulled from my side.

"All right," I said and watched the faintest light of hope stir in his eyes again. "We'll find another way for you … keep you out of the worst of it." He met my eyes at last, and I felt myself shudder at the concession I'd made, hoping it wouldn't cost me the last edge I'd need … hoping it wouldn't cost me the war. "I won't make you kill anyone like that again."

Chapter 35

I was deep in the dreamwalk; the bridging, undefined space in my head that I used to contact people while I was sleeping. It was a dark, smoky realm based on a shared memory, the lines of the space wisping like smoke.

I was in a wide-open office space, standing right in the middle of it. The desks had been cleared out, and open floor stood between me and the other person in the dreamwalk. He was looking around in mild surprise, but only mild. I'd been hoping he'd be stunned to be here, but I hadn't given him enough credit for being jaded.

"Is this London?" Weissman said, his greasy black hair ringing his face. "The Omega offices?"

"Well, we did meet there last time we crossed paths," I said, staring at him across the room. There was no sound but that of our voices when they broke the unearthly silence. "Though I can change things up if you'd prefer." I snapped my fingers and we stood in a sunlit atrium, a white glow emanating from every surface.

"The British Museum?" Weissman said, cocking his head to look around. "Quite the little talent you've got for settings. I take it this is a dreamwalk?"

"You don't seem surprised."

"Sovereign told me about it," Weissman said, still looking around. A grin split his face, revealing yellowed teeth. "This is where I killed the Omega ministers. Good times. Any chance you can take me to some of my other greatest hits? Because there was this one time in a parking lot—"

"How's your week going, Weissman?" I asked, preempting

what I was sure was going to be a fascinating tale of grossness and murder. Why were the villains in my life so damned villainous? Why couldn't I just face off with bullying toe-rags who wanted to embarrass you like a normal nineteen-year-old? Instead, I had the League of Evil trying to kill all the metahumans in the world to contend with.

"You threw a few kinks in it," he said, smiling through an obvious grimace. "I gotta admit, I didn't see you finding one of our active safe houses, let alone busting down the door gangster-style and laying waste to everyone inside. It was an embarrassing oversight on my part."

"Yeah, I can see how losing thirteen of your hundred like that would fall into the 'embarrassing' category," I said with all due sarcasm.

He reddened. "That wasn't so smart. You made me look stupid in front of Sovereign."

"I didn't 'make' you look stupid," I said. "You are stupid. I just gave you the opportunity to showcase it."

"Ooh." He let a little air pass through his lips as he narrowed his eyes, the mark of a suppressed fury. "Are you being snide and condescending?"

"And here I was, worried you were too stupid to pick up on it."

He laughed, but it was a mirthless, mean-spirited guffaw. "I already have your people marked down for a hell of a violent death, did you know that? But I'm brainstorming more creative ways to make them suffer before they die every time you throw a wrench in my plans. I'm up to vivisection and acid baths, in case you're wondering."

"Well, gosh, I guess I should just surrender now and make their deaths easier and marginally less painful."

He made a tsk-ing sound and smiled. "You're trying to get my goat. Trying to make me say something … unwise."

"I would never try to get your goat," I said. "I'd hate to deprive you of your only outlet for sexual release."

"Oh, wow." He blanched in annoyance, "I'd forgotten how incredibly irritating you are. Did you just summon me here to dig a deeper grave for all those hangers-on you laughably call your friends? Or was it because you missed me?"

"I do miss how easy it is to make a mockery of you," I said. "I'm afforded so very few truly witless targets to spin in circles with my derision. But I wouldn't say I miss you—in fact, last time I'm pretty sure I hit you to the tune of a gaping stomach wound. Maybe soon I'll have another opportunity to test my aim on you." I took a step closer to him. "You can threaten me and my friends all you want. I know you want to kill them. I know you're going to try and make it painful. And out there in the real world, you have lots of power backing you up." I disappeared in a wisp of smoke and appeared again behind him. "But here … you're in my world. Let me show you who has the power here."

I clamped a hand on his face and he screamed. It was a wrenching, gut-level cry of agony. "I can manipulate the dream world, Weissman." I brought him to his knees, screaming in anguish all the while. "I can find you anytime you go to sleep. I can torment you every night from here until I die." I circled around him, looking in his dark eyes. "I can wrench every ounce of happiness out of your life and make it hell until the very end, and I suspect I'll be living a lot longer than you will, however this turns out."

"You … little … bitch …" His words were choked out, and he was on his knees. I shaped a thought and filled the air with the smell of urine.

"That's just sad," I said. Because I was shaping the world, it was real to him. For all I knew, it was reflecting life and he'd wake up to a wet bed. "I know you're committed to this little war of yours, but I don't think you realize how committed I am. You better start sleeping during the day, Weissman." I knelt next to him. "Because I'm going to haunt your dreams every night for the rest of your life."

He glared at me. "No … you're not."

There was a screaming, flaring pain in my head as something broke through the bright white walls of the dream. Everything went red and I found myself on my knees in an agony of my own.

"Bet you thought you had me there for a minute," Weissman said. His sadistic glee had returned. "But that was dumb on your part. Because if you think I hadn't considered the possibility you would try this very thing, you'd be WRONG." He raised his voice on the last bit. "You feel that pain?" There was a shocking agony in the front of my head, radiating out like fire in my brain. "That's a telepath, stepping into your little dreamwalk. It's your friend Claire from Vegas, and I think she's still a little upset that you broke her leg the way you did."

"I should have killed her," I mumbled as the pain surged again.

"I think you'll be regretting that choice before the end," Weissman said with a laugh. "Because now I've still got two active telepaths outside of your betrothed, Sovereign, to finish this job." He leered down at me. "And we're going to finish this job. All the way to the bloody end." He grinned. "But first, I think it might be best if we put you in a coma for a week or two. Give you a chance to ponder how badly you've failed—and give you time to wonder—and fear—what you might wake up to. Claire?" He snapped his fingers. "Make her a Brussels sprout for a while."

I tensed my body, looking up at him as he stared down at me. I tried to brace myself, as though there was some way to protect myself against whatever psychic assault was coming.

Weissman held there for a minute, still, before speaking again. "Claire?"

"Oh, I don't think she'll be joining us right now," came a deep, sonorous voice from behind me. I turned to see Dr. Zollers standing behind me. "I've cut her out of the conversation for the time being."

"Zollers," Weissman said with a seething fury. "You were the worst mistake we ever made." He pointed a finger at the doctor. "And when I catch up with you, I'm gonna take a lot longer with you than I have with anyone else. You will suffer for weeks. I'll open up your skull and pull out pieces of your brain just to find out which parts are the psychic ones. Then—"

"You're welcome to try, of course," Zollers said. "But thanks to your efforts—and hers," he gave a slight nod to me, "I'm now the most powerful telepath on the planet, so you'll have a hell of a time restraining my mental energies enough to experiment." He paused. "I think you're about to be shaken awake; allow me to give you a parting gift—something to remember me by until we meet again."

Weissman screamed with a fury and pain that made what I'd done to him sound like the work of an amateur gently pinging him on the knee with a reflex hammer. This agony was full and deep, and it sounded like his soul was being shredded as he cried out in such utter anguish that the world shattered around me from the strength of his screams.

I awoke in the dark, in my bed, the faint light of the campus shining in beyond my window. I lay there, frozen, tucked beneath the sheets in a cold sweat, another avenue closed off. I sat there until I got my breathing under control, gasps of fear coming one after another.

It took hours. And I never got back to sleep.

Chapter 36

I bumped into Kat the next morning while I was shouldering my way into the ladies' room nearest my office. I was in a hurry, had a full staff meeting in five minutes. I heard her making a kind of thumping noise while I was in the stall, but I ignored it. When I emerged, she was standing there in front of the mirrors, sucking in her cheeks.

"Why the hell are you making fish faces in the mirror?" I asked her.

"What?" She turned toward me. Now she was making a duck face, her full, pouty lips flattened at me.

"Bang. Bang," I said, making a gun with my thumb and forefinger.

"What was that for?" Her expression turned to a full-on frown.

"You were making a duck face," I said.

"Fish face, duck face? I have no idea what you're talking about." She got a pouty look that somehow fell between the two and looked back in the mirror. "Do I look old to you, Sienna?"

"You look eighteen," I said. "Just like you always have." I didn't mention that she acted twelve, because it didn't seem like the right time for it.

"It's just … Janus. He's so different since he woke up," she said, staring at herself in the mirror. "So … preoccupied."

"Maybe he's worried about being exterminated," I suggested, a little lightly.

"Maybe," she conceded. "Things just feel so different. I was worrying that maybe I was starting to look my age."

I wondered how she had survived so long, being as thoroughly non-serious a person as she was. Then again, I wasn't exactly super-serious all the time myself. "Don't be ridiculous. Most girls who have hit a centennial would be lucky to have skin like yours. Because you don't have any wrinkles. At all. And honestly, the way you grin all the time like a—" I stopped myself before saying moron, "—very happy person, that's a good thing. You look fine."

"Thank you, Sienna," she turned to me, and I realized I'd just offered encouragement to her. I felt a little dirty, like I'd just crawled around on the floor of a girl's locker room at high school. "That's very sweet of you to say."

I gagged on the responses I came up with, trying to remember that she probably considered sweetness a virtue or something. "Meeting?" I asked, smiling faintly through the wave of nausea.

"Oh, yeah, right," she said and led the way to the conference room. She bubbled the whole way there, and I nodded in time with her comments, saying, "Sure," at the appropriate intervals.

Once we were all situated in the conference room, the air heavy with the smell of all the coffee cups lining the table, I started off with an explanation of what had happened with Weissman in the dreamwalk. When I was finished, I waited for someone to respond.

"So you were just going to badger the hell out of him in his dreams for the rest of his life?" Reed asked.

"It seemed like a good way to get under his skin," I replied.

"But dangerous," my mother said. "I had no idea we were vulnerable in a dreamwalk like that."

"Yeah, it's a good thing Dr. Zollers was looking out for me," I said, and glanced his way.

Zollers, for his part, seemed immobile. "It was a fortunate bit of timing on my part. Next time, perhaps warn me if you're planning something of that sort? I could have intervened sooner if I'd known what was going on. As it was, I had to sense your emotional distress from a few floors away. Interrupted a perfectly good dream about a beach on Tahiti."

"What's the next move?" Scott asked somewhat listlessly from his place down the table. He was leaned back in his chair, clad entirely in his navy pullover and blue jeans. He looked good, but tired.

"I believe I have an answer for that," Janus said, and I could see the twinkle in his eye.

"J.J. found something down your money trail?" I asked.

"Indeed," Janus said. "Safe houses all over the United States. There is an advance buyer who is picking up rental locations in the cities where they next plan to stage. Several of the landlords photocopied the driver's license of this person." He took a page out of the folder sitting in front of him and slid it to me. "I asked J.J. how to use the projector to put it on the wall, but … I am afraid it is a bit beyond my capabilities, so he offered me a Xerox instead."

I looked at the face on the paper. It was a young guy, probably in his twenties, smiling in the license photo. "Doesn't look familiar."

"I had Agent Li run him through your FBI's database," Janus said.

"No priors," Li said, almost bored, "no record. He's squeaky clean."

"False identity?" Reed asked.

"Probably not," Li said. "I think he's legit. Metas don't tend to have many run-ins with the law. You all run too fast to get cornered by law enforcement." He shot a daggered look at me on that one.

"So we've got a buyer," I said. "We have some safe houses … how many?"

"About six at present," Janus said. "San Francisco, Los Angeles, San Diego, Brooklyn, Atlanta and Tulsa."

"Whoa. Which one of these things is not like the others?" Reed asked.

"Why Tulsa?" my mother asked. "That is … odd."

"You think it could be their headquarters or something?" I asked.

"Unlikely," Janus said, glancing up. "The Tulsa rental is a storage unit. A small space, something on the order of a five-foot by five-foot space in a warehouse."

I made the frowniest of frowny faces. "What the hell? What would they be keeping in a storage unit in Tulsa?"

"I don't know, but I kind of want to find out," Reed said. "What's the likelihood it's something dangerous in a space that small?"

I swept my eyes from my mother to Janus, the two most experienced people at the table. "What would you think it would be?"

"Could be a conventional weapon of some sort," my mother said. "Biological, chemical, nuclear or radiological. Doesn't seem like it'd be a meta—at least not a live one—in that small of a space. Unless they're a prisoner of some sort."

"FBI could handle conventional weapons," I said.

"We ought to be your first choice for handling those types of threats," Li said stiffly, "since I doubt any of you know how to deal with weapons of mass destruction."

"Fine," I said diplomatically. "Why don't you have your people crack open that storage unit? Warn them to be careful, give them the heads up that it could be anything—after all, we have no idea what Century is planning for the human race after they get done with us. This could be their phase two." I lapsed into a silence after that, staring at the table.

"What?" Ariadne asked, breaking the silence. She was a little brusque about it.

"Well, now we've got a direction," I said. "But I'm not sure how much it helps us."

"We have enemies to destroy, do we not?" Janus asked. "I

spoke before about executing lightning raids, and now we have targets. Imagine we could hit these five safe houses and eliminate some thirty or forty Century operatives in the process. We would have them down to less than half strength. If you can't call that a victory, I don't know what you could."

"But they're going to get tougher, aren't they?" I stared evenly at Janus. "You know some of what they have available, don't you? How easy will it be for us to continue to roll through a Century safe house and not take casualties?"

Janus paused. "I think you would have to expect some casualties from an operation of this kind. There is simply no way around it. Not going against the people you will be facing. I believe they have recruited very powerful metas and you will begin to run across some of them as time goes on. However, they are not invincible."

I blinked. "Wolfe was nearly invincible."

"Nearly," Janus said, "but, as you proved, not. Even the most powerful metas have weaknesses. They can all be beaten."

"Maybe," I said, stroking my chin. "In most cases, we don't know what we'll be facing. In one case, at least, we do. Weissman." I stared around the table. "And I don't know how to beat him."

"Have your telepath grind his brain's gears so he can't zoom around," Scott said, shrugging from where he slumped in his chair, "then shoot him in the face. You're good at that." He paused. "I'm not trying to be snotty, I actually mean it. You're a good shot."

"That would be a lot easier if he didn't have a telepath of his own to block me," Zollers said.

"I thought you said you were the strongest." I froze, watching the doctor.

"I am," Zollers said calmly, "but this Claire—she's no slouch. I can beat her, but she'll keep me busy for a few minutes, and that's all the time Weissman needs if I understand his powers correctly."

"You beat him before," my mother said. "How did you do it in London?"

"Overwhelmed him with the numbers," I said. "It was five on one, and I had Breandan's luck on my side along with Karthik's illusions to distract him."

"Yeah, I didn't fling him through the air or anything," Reed said sourly.

"Plus Reed," I said. "But those other two helped a lot."

"We'll need to choose a battlefield that's to our advantage," my mother said, all business.

"There's no battlefield to our advantage, not against Weissman," I said. How do you beat a man who could control the very flow of time itself? "If only we had someone else on our side that could do what he—" A knock at the door interrupted me. "Who is it?"

Kurt popped his acne-scarred face in the door. I could tell by his expression that whatever he had to say, it was not good. "We have a security breach."

"What?" I was on my feet in an instant. "What happened?"

"Security cameras caught footage of a man appearing and disappearing on the monitors just now," he said, opening the door the rest of the way.

"Weissman," I said, and looked around the room, as though I could feel him hiding.

Kurt's face took on a pained expression. "Based on the description you gave us … I don't think it's that guy. This one … he's … uh … Asian in origin."

I frowned. "Weissman's not Asian."

"Bang-up observational skills there," Reed said from behind me. "He's a white guy. A white guy with long, greasy black hair."

"Right, well, this gentleman had short hair, and he was Asian," Kurt said. I could feel the discomfort radiating off of him, as though he were uncomfortable so much as describing the racial characteristics of the intruder in front of Li. I could tell because he wouldn't even look at Li as he was speaking.

"Where was the intruder last sighted?" I asked, brushing past Kurt to look over the cubicle farm.

"Just outside your office," Kurt said.

I took off at a run, and heard voices of protest behind me in the conference room. I didn't care; if this guy could appear and disappear at will, it didn't matter if I faced him alone. I was overmatched no matter what. The cubicles blurred past as I ran around the perimeter of the open floor until I reached my office door. It was open just a crack and I pushed it, the hinges squeaking.

I stared inside, and the first thing I noticed was the one thing that had most definitely not been there when last I'd been here.

"What the hell, Sienna?" Scott came to a halt behind me, Reed and my mother only steps behind him. "Are you crazy?"

"No," I said and edged toward my desk one slow step at a time.

"I don't see anyone," Reed said from the doorway, looking around.

"I think he's gone," I said, and took the last step to my desk.

"What makes you say that?" Scott asked.

"Because he left something behind," I said, staring down at the object on my desk.

"Well, don't—" my mother started to say, but it was too late.

I picked up the white envelope laid against the base of the bonsai tree's pot. The bonsai was just sitting there in the middle of my desk, perfectly aligned. Someone had spent time positioning it. They had left the envelope leaning in front, and it had my name written across it.

"That could have anything in it," my mother said, sounding like a cross between a mother and paranoid FBI agent. I slid my finger under the seal of the envelope and opened it. "Anthrax, anyone?"

"Does that fall into the category of diseases and infections we're immune to?" Reed asked as I slid the note from the envelope and read it once. Then again. "Well, don't keep us in suspense," he said after a minute, "what's it say?"

I blinked and read it quietly one more time. "It says, 'To Sienna Nealon: I am in your debt. I will be at the Japanese Garden at Como Park Conservatory tonight at nine p.m. Won't you speak with me?'"

"Well, that doesn't sound like a trap at all," Reed said. "You're not going, of course."

"I am going," I said. I could feel the tautness in my chest. The timing was … fanciful. But then, if it was him, time was his plaything, so it would make sense that he'd know his help was needed, and now. "I have to."

"Wow, I was pretty sure my sane sister walked in here, but now she's gone and there's a crazy person in her place," Reed said. "Why would you even consider taking a mystery invitation from someone that's made it appear in your office?" He took a couple steps toward me to look over my shoulder. "Does it even say who it's from?"

"Yeah, it's signed," I said. I stared at the elegant, flowing handwriting that was exquisite in its detail. Just like the perfectly aligned plant on my desk. "It's signed, 'Shin'ichi Akiyama.'"

"Random person asks you to meet in a darkened garden at night, you leap at the invitation," Reed said. "I know you had an unconventional upbringing," he grinned at my mom, who stood staring into the office quietly, eyes fixed on the bonsai, "but I would think that you'd have learned a good, healthy fear of strangers—"

"He's not a stranger." I looked up from the invitation, staring at each of them in turn. "Not really. Shin'ichi Akiyama … is the only man Weissman has ever feared."

Chapter 37

Night had fallen, and I was sitting in a van outside the Como Park Conservatory. It was a massive glass structure that extended a hundred feet into the air in a dome shape, with greenhouse-shaped protrusions jutting out from the center dome like spokes from a hub. White metal struts separated each pane of glass. It was lit from the outside, and the beautiful setting made me wonder what it was like in the daytime.

"The Japanese garden is outside," my mother said, a little quietly. She had been sedate all day, ever since the security breach. I had expected a more vocal debate from her, the way I'd gotten it from pretty much everyone else, but she'd been virtually silent about the whole thing.

"Does anyone else think this is capital-C crazy?" Reed asked from the driver's seat. Scott was sitting next to him, and nodded along without saying anything. "Okay, I just wanted to make sure I hadn't had a psychotic break with reality."

Dr. Zollers was sitting in the seat just behind me and had said almost as little as my mother had. "Are you sure you want to do this?" To his credit, he didn't try to discourage me. At least, I thought it was to his credit. If he was walking me into a trap, I might not find it nearly so creditable.

"I'm sure," I said, unfastening my seat belt. "Just wait here."

"Um, no," Reed said, "we're going in with you."

"Akiyama invited me," I said. "To bring others feels … rude, somehow."

"Really?" Reed asked. "Because to me it feels insane to do otherwise. You're talking about walking into an uncontrolled setting while we're at war, and you're going to do so while keeping your backup a few hundred feet away." His eyes grew dark. "This is the sort of thing I'd expect from someone who's too stupid to live, not from you, my normally tactically smart sister."

I felt my stomach rumble and knew he was right; yet for some reason, I knew I had to do this. There was something about the invitation from Akiyama, as crazy as it sounded, that told me I needed to accept. I'd looked at the security footage, and there was something … familiar about him. He'd looked straight at the camera, and his face … I'd trusted him instantly for some reason I couldn't define. Something inside told me that I needed to be here, right now. This was an opportunity that we desperately needed. If Akiyama would help us, and we could kill Weissman …

… the war would be over. Not even Sovereign could stand against Akiyama's power. Not after we had removed all of Century's support mechanism from beneath him.

"Why did the invitation say he was in your debt?" Scott asked. He'd been nitpicking this point for hours.

I still didn't have an answer for him. "I have no idea." I glanced at my cell phone, letting the faceplate light the van in the dark. The only other light was being shed from the streetlights around us.

"Does that not bother you?" Reed said. "I don't see how you can be so calm when everything about this stinks—"

"I don't know!" I said, sighing. "I don't know, okay? Every minute we're in this fight with Century, I question myself. Did I make the right moves the day they raided our dorm and killed all those people? Was I a fool to turn down Erich Winter's offer of help before he died? Did I screw up majorly by not just accepting my fate and killing Bjorn when Winter told me to?" I lowered my voice. "Am I a fool for not going to Sovereign now and telling him I'll marry him and do whatever he wants if he'll call off this extermination?"

Reed started to interrupt but I shushed him. "My life is a train on a track right now. Most people get to make a million choices every day, from the inconsequential to the important, choices that steer their lives. I've got one big one—should I fight Century or run? And a thousand tactical decisions to make from there that will lead to one of two basic outcomes—we'll either win or we'll lose. And if we lose, you'll all die."

"Which is why I can't figure out why you're making this choice right now!" Reed's pent-up fury exploded out of him. "This smells like a setup. Like an ambush. Like you're just leading us right into the mouth of the lion so we can get good and dead quicker than we would otherwise. We have a plan. We could hit those safe houses, start wiping Century off the map—"

"You're missing it," I said with a faint smile. It was mournful, not mirthful. "If we do that, we accomplish one thing—we winnow their numbers down from the one hundred they had when they started. But they're gonna take everything they have left and throw it at us at that point. They may already be moving to do that."

"Then we fight them!" Reed said. "I like fifty or forty or thirty to eight odds better than I like eighty to eight. If they're gonna come, let's do some damage first."

I shook my head. "And that's the point. We can't win the war that way. Even if we grind them down to thirty to eight—assuming no one dies on the raids—we'll be able to take out maybe another ten of them before we go down." I felt all expression leave my face. "And then the rest will just move on with their plan. Wipe humanity off the board, or whatever they're going to do. The way we are currently playing the game, we … will … lose." I hit every word with extra emphasis. "It's inevitable. Like destiny."

"So instead we just throw the game away right now," Scott said with a scornful sigh.

"No," I said. "We hedge a long-odds bet. And it is long odds,

I'll be the first to admit it. Akiyama is coming to us at an insanely convenient time, if he's really coming to help us. But I'm willing to risk a trap—a confrontation—if it will give us a chance to change our fate. Because I see where we're going, how this war is going to play out for us … and I can't …" My voice broke. "I can't do it. I know you think I'm cold and heartless, but I can't stand by and lose you all one by one in attrition through raids then watch while Weissman rallies everything they have left so he can inflict painful and punishing deaths on each of you in turn."

I shook my head and my hand found the handle for the van's door. "Scott, Reed … wait here. Keep your eyes peeled."

"Sure, suicide guard duty sounds like fun," Reed said, sullen.

"I don't want you to be on suicide guard duty," I said. "If you see trouble coming … I want you to run."

There was a silence in the van. "Are you freaking kidding me?" Reed asked. He turned his head all the way around to look at me. "You think I'm going to run?"

"You were just arguing tactics with me," I said. "What sense does it make to throw all of our lives away in an ambush?"

"Slightly more sense than it makes to walk into the ambush in the first place," Reed said hotly. "If you die, we're done. Do you realize that?"

"No, you're not," I said, shaking my head. "I've got nothing extra to offer the cause except the skills my mother taught me."

"You have the power—"

"I don't," I said with a sigh. "I don't. If it's in me somewhere … I don't know how to use it. However Sovereign does it … I don't know how to do it. My souls hate me. The one thing they have in common is that. They don't want to help me; they want to see me die for what I've done to them. I can't figure out how to force them to give me their power. I've tried. I can't get them to so much as give me a moment's assistance …" I bowed my head.

"I'm just another soldier, Reed. Which is why I'm willing to take this gamble."

Reed pursed his lips tight. Scott sat next to him, refusing to even look back at me. "Stay in the van," I told them. Reed grudgingly nodded. "Run at the first sign of trouble. I need to talk to Zollers, and then I'll send him back to you so he can warn you if something comes this way."

I opened the door to the van and stepped out into the brisk, pre-autumnal evening. I held the door open as my mother joined me wordlessly, and then Zollers followed from the back seat. I slammed the door and listened to the finality of the sound as it echoed over the empty road.

"Do I need to say it?" I asked Zollers as he fell into step beside me. We were walking along a concrete sidewalk toward a gate at the far end of the building.

"You want me to coerce them into leaving if things get hot," Zollers said in his usual, mild sort of way. "I'll try. They're both struggling under the burden of strong emotions that would be driving them in the opposite direction. At least, Reed is. Scott ..." He shook his head.

"He's a mess," I said.

"I've seen worse," Zollers said. "He's haunted by that experience in Vegas. I've counseled people through similar things, and I think I can bring him around, given some time."

"Time ..." I said, staring over the gate. I knew the Japanese Garden was over there somewhere. "Let's hope I can get us some of that."

"The man waiting over there *is* Shin'ichi Akiyama," Zollers said, "or at least he believes he is. I can read that much." He smiled. "Assuming you believe my word."

"I believe you," I said, and I did. "You haven't steered me wrong yet. Warning me not to trust anyone at the Directorate, trying to guide me from a world away, sending me the visions of Adelaide so I could find that secret room in Omega Headquarters—" I froze as his face bore a deep frown. "What?"

"I don't know what you're talking about in relation to this … Adelaide?" Zollers said, his face creased with uncertainty. "I never gave you any visions that I know of. I just tried to keep an eye on your psyche, help keep you as stable as possible from afar. I have no idea who 'Adelaide' is."

I blinked, trying to rack my brain. "But … I was having these visions in London, and I was sure you gave them to me. How else would—?"

"It's almost nine o'clock," my mother said, a little abruptly, from beside me. "We need to get you to your meeting."

I cast a last look back at Zollers, who was already retreating back toward the van. "Please," I said.

"I will do what I can," he said.

"Come on," my mother said, more than a little tense. I could feel the tension radiating from her in a way I couldn't recall ever experiencing before. She jogged toward the gate and leapt over it with one good jump. I followed and landed on the pavement with all the delicacy of a kid playing hopscotch.

"That's a little weird, isn't it?" I asked my mother as I shot one last look back to Zollers. "I had these visions, fully-formed, of a succubus who worked for Omega in the eighties, and—"

"That's a little weird," my mother said, cutting me off as she led the way up the path.

"What's wrong with you?" I asked as we veered off the road onto a path. Plants and bushes surrounded the path, well-tended greenery that marked the start of the garden.

"Nothing," she said, not turning to face me. She kept on, a couple paces ahead.

"Something's up," I said, and hurried to catch her. I matched her stride and looked at her face. It was all seriousness.

The path turned slightly left, and I could hear water running ahead. A still pond lay on our right, and my mother stopped without warning. "I'm going to wait here," she said. Her face was shrouded in darkness. There were few lights here, only a couple lamps shining in the darkness. The tranquility oozed over the scene, and I noticed leaves crunching underfoot for the first time as I came to a halt.

"Okay," I said. "Why do I get the feeling you're betraying me?"

She stood partially in the shadows, and I heard a faint sigh. "I assure you I'm not. But … before you go …"

"Oh, boy," I said. "Don't say goodbye or I'll really think you've walked me into a trap."

She didn't move, the shadows of the overhead branches hiding her expression. "I wanted to tell you … I'm sorry."

I looked around, turning my head in a slow circle. "Seriously, is Weissman going to come jumping out at me right now?"

"No," she said, a little cautiously. "But I need to tell you something."

"Maybe you could start by explaining what you're sorry for," I said, eyeing her more than a little warily. My paranoia was in full swing, even though I knew—somehow—that I was supposed to be here.

"I'm sorry for what I put you through," she said. "I'm sorry it was necessary. I'm sorry I locked you in the box all those years. I'm sorry I wasn't strong enough, wasn't smart enough, to see any other way to keep you safe." I couldn't see her face in the shadows. "I'm sorry I had to break your spirit to keep you down. And most of all … I'm sorry you couldn't live a normal life."

I was still looking sideways every few seconds, waiting for something to come jumping out at me. When it didn't come, I took a step toward her in the shadows. Now I could see her face, faintly, and it looked … contrite. "It wasn't your fault I couldn't have a normal life," I said. What else was I supposed to say? "And

… I don't know. I don't know what else to say to any of the rest of that except … your timing sucks."

"What?" She looked up at me. "Oh. Right. Well. I felt like it needed to be said, and if I waited I might never say it."

"Yeah … kind of ominous the way you laid that out right now, but …" I didn't even know if I honestly wanted an apology from her at this point. We'd come to a place where we could deal with each other independently of the past, and it felt a lot better to just leave my childhood where it lay. "Anyway. I'm off to meet my fate."

"What?" She looked up at me, genuine confusion hidden by the lines of the shadows.

"Gonna see if we have an ally or an ambush," I said. "You gonna wait here for me?"

"I'll be waiting," she said, and the tension was back in her voice. "Take as long as you need."

My head was spinning from what my mother had said, and her timing in saying it. I felt like I was suspicious of everything at this point, like the whole world could be conspiring against me. Really, if Sovereign could change his face, I probably wasn't wrong to be as suspicious as I was. Still, it was … disconcerting to be thinking that way all the time.

I drew a deep breath of the fresh garden air as I followed the path around another curve. The sound of water flowing was louder here, and I could see a lamp burning ahead next to a piece of stonework that had a top shaped like a pagoda.

I rounded a corner and saw a waterfall flowing down a massive stone ledge into a little stream below. It burbled as it ran, drowning out the distant sounds of the city at night.

There was a bench next to the stream, and I could see the silhouette of a man sitting upon it, his posture stiff and straight, as though he were a statue. I could see his face lit by the lamp overhead. He wore a suit and looked exactly like he had on the security monitor. He had a goatee speckled with salt and pepper, but the hair on his head was a deep jet black. He stood as I approached, my quiet footsteps ringing out in the night as obvious as gunshots would be to a human.

When I got close, he bent into a deep bow, very formally. When he came back up, I aped his motion but less deeply because I wanted to keep an eye on him. He watched me all the while, and when I finished, he spoke.

"It is a pleasure to see you again, Sienna Nealon," he said, inclining his head. "I am Shin'ichi Akiyama."

"I'm sorry. Did you see me before?" I asked. "When you were at my office this morning?"

"No," he said with a subtle shake of his head. "I merely dropped off my humble gift—which I hope you find pleasing—and withdrew to return here for contemplation."

"I'm sorry, but you said it was a pleasure to see me *again*," I said, something troubling me. "That usually implies that you've seen me before."

"Indeed," he said, tilting his head once more in acknowledgment. "My grasp of English is not as flawless as it perhaps could be. I believe the proper way to say what I had intended was, 'It is a pleasure to meet you again.'"

I wondered if this was a communication problem. "I'm sorry, I don't think that's right. We haven't met before."

He seemed to take a deep breath in through the nose. "Ah, but I believe you are mistaken. For you see, I have most assuredly encountered the great Sienna Nealon in my past."

"I … that's just confusing," I said. "I'm pretty sure I would remember you if we'd met before."

He smiled and bowed his head once more. The wind stirred through the trees, loud enough to make itself obvious over the sounds of the babbling brook running beside us. Akiyama took a deep breath, and when he spoke, it seemed as though the world held its breath for just a second to let him say his piece. “I assure you, I am just as certain that I could not forget Sienna Nealon … the Girl in the Box.”

Chapter 38

"What did you just call me?" I asked. I had flashed a little with anger at what he'd said.

"Are you familiar with the Japanese concept of *hakoiri musume*?" he asked, studying me with penetrating eyes. His whole posture was restful, placid. As though the world was flowing around him like he was one of the stones in the stream next to us. "Translated it means something akin to 'daughter in a box.' A girl protected and sheltered from the world around her."

I felt my jaw tighten, my teeth clench together. "You seem to know an awful lot more about me than I know about you."

"Forgive my lack of subtlety," he said with another nod of his head. "I wished to demonstrate my familiarity with you, not insult you."

"I'm not insulted, exactly," I said, a little taken aback. "Just … surprised … that you might have heard some details of my upbringing that I didn't know were exactly public knowledge."

"You should not be surprised, as you told me of your upbringing yourself," he said, never taking his eyes off me.

"I did not …" I paused. "I haven't met you until just now … but you know me."

"Indeed I know you," he said, and I caught a slight smile from him, "and I am in your debt."

Something occurred to me, and a little chill ran through me that wasn't from the night air. "We've met … else-when."

"And elsewhere," Akiyama said. "Something you would not know … there are two of me in this time period. One here, speaking with you, and another … on an island not far from Nagasaki." He remained still for a moment as I processed my way through what he had just said. “Did you know that Nagasaki is a sister city to your own St. Paul?”

“I … did not,” I said, my head still spinning.

“Indeed,” he said. “It is why this garden is here.”

I thought about it. “How did you know that Nagasaki was a sister city to St. Paul?”

He smiled. “Because you told me when last I met you.”

“God, I have a headache,” I said, and I really felt like I did. Possible betrayals and paranoia were nothing next to the confusion of time travel that he’d just opened up on me. “So … what you’re saying is that I’ll meet you again, someday in my future?”

“Someday,” he said. “And on that day, you will do me the greatest service one could ever ask of another. It is that kindness that has placed me in your debt.”

“Well, that’s … great,” I said. “Since you’re in my debt, I need some help.”

He glanced at me, only briefly, before turning his attention back to the waterfall. “Weissman.”

“He’s a big problem,” I said. “Him and Century, if you’re familiar with them.”

“You have told me all about them,” he said, but now he wasn’t looking at me. “I know what you would ask of me, but I am afraid my ability to intervene in this time is … limited by circumstance.”

I felt all the air leave my lungs. “You just said you were in my debt. You just told me that I would do you the greatest service or favor or something that could ever be asked. I’m fighting a war here, and I could really use your help.”

He looked back at me, and I could see a cocked eyebrow. “I know all of this. But you do not understand. My hands are tied when I am in this place.”

“Because there’s another you in this time?” I felt my head wanting to ache again. It wasn’t really aching, but it felt like it should be. “Because—”

"I cannot interfere because in the manner which you would have me act," he said, gently speaking over me, "because it would destroy all that would follow after." He turned to face me. "Time is a river, and I may traverse in either direction. However, I cannot divert the stream in whatever manner I choose. I can only tread the water that is there. What has happened before must happen again."

I felt the air of hope that I'd begun to feel slowly seep out of me. "Then why are you here? If you can't help me, why would you come here now?"

"Because I am in your debt, Sienna Nealon," he said, speaking slowly.

"What good is your debt to me if you're not going to settle up?" I asked, and I was pretty sure my frustration was leaking out all over the place. "What point is there to you owing me something if you won't deliver what I need?"

He kept his face utterly devoid of emotion. "Just because I am not repaying my debt to you in the manner that you choose right now, do not assume that I will let it go unpaid. I bring you a warning—Weissman is here."

I stiffened. "In Minneapolis?"

"He approaches this place even now," Akiyama said seriously. "His telepath is tracking you and would have led him directly to your campus on this night were you not here instead."

"What?" I felt the stirrings of alarm. "You could have told me earlier—"

"We do not have much time," he said seriously, and the part of me that wanted to throttle him stood by listening, instead, as he spelled out the horror that was rushing my way even now. "He has with him two others besides the telepath. They are two of his strongest, and they will be familiar to you."

"I have to go," I said, and started to turn away from him.

Akiyama grabbed my hand and held it firm as I tried to pull away. "Sienna Nealon," he said, catching my attention. I looked back at him, wanting to pull my hand away and run, run so I could warn my mother and the others. "Your destiny will be decided this night." The seconds ticked by, and he looked in my eyes with great significance, significance I did not understand. "However you might feel, you are walking your own path through the darkness. Do not despair when all the light leaves you, and remember your past—it will see you through the trials ahead."

"Thanks for nothing," I said and ripped my hand out of his grasp. I had felt the stirrings of my power start to work on him as he spoke, but he showed little sign that it had affected him at all. With one last look, I saw him watching me as I broke into a sprint back down the path toward my mother. I wanted to cry. I wanted to scream.

But instead, I locked my jaw in place and ran, ran as hard as I could down the dark path through the garden.

Chapter 39

"Come on!" I shouted at mom as I passed, and I heard her break into a run behind me. The quiet of the night was shattered by the pounding of our feet. I barely noticed the greenery of the garden around me. Where it had felt peaceful only moments earlier, now I felt nothing of the sort as the branches and boughs streaked by. A screaming urgency was tearing at me from deep within, willing me forward to the frightening reality waiting for me just outside.

I jumped over the gate and was running again as I heard my mother land behind me. I sprinted for the van, and saw Zollers open the door and step out as I approached. "Get in!" I shouted. "They're coming!"

"I can't sense them," Zollers said, his face muted alarm. "I can't …" His eyes widened. "Oh God. They're close. She's—" His neck cranked around and I saw a flash as a car appeared—literally appeared, out of thin air—behind the van. The doors opened and two huge figures unfolded themselves from the front seat.

"Weissman used his power to get them here without you being able to detect him," I said. "Sneak attack."

"Cornered, I'd call it," my mother said from behind me. "Can we run?"

"They can appear anywhere we go," Zollers said. "They can follow us in an instant."

"Well, well, well," Weissman said, appearing from behind the headlights of the car. He was still flanked by the two big guys, but I could see Claire's shorter figure next to him. "Guess who's got the power here, Sienna?"

"Probably Xcel Energy," I smarted off. Scott and Reed were out of the van now as well, and they all followed behind me as I shuffled to stand in the light of Weissman's car's headlights.

"Always with the witty retort," Weissman said, grinning. "But I think it's pretty obvious who's got the power now. You run, we run you down. You fight, things go badly for you. You're the mouse, I'm the cat—and by the end of tonight, even you, you dense, snotty little bitch—you'll get the picture." He turned his head to look at Scott. "Well, well. If it isn't the little Byerly brat. Isn't this a plus?"

"Excuse me?" Scott asked. "Do I know you?" He asked way more politely than I would have, like he was at a formal soirée and being introduced to a society gentleman or something.

"No," Weissman said with a grin. "But I knew your aunt and uncle. For, like … years. In fact, it was me that killed them. Don't know if you knew that."

"Bullshit," Scott said. "Wolfe killed my aunt and uncle."

"Au contraire, you stupid dipshit," Weissman said, still smiling. "It was me. But I can see why you'd think it was Wolfe. It did happen around the time he was ripping through the city here. Gave me a nice cover to settle an old score and kick off the extermination while ending a personal grudge on a sweet, bloody note."

I remembered back to what Wolfe had said to me in the basement, just before he and I fought for the last time, something about how someone else was joining in on his good times.

"You son of a bitch," Scott breathed. He sounded like he was having trouble getting his words out. "You son of a …"

"Ooh," Claire said, taunting, "I think you just gave the water boy some motivation to fight. Seems he'd lost his fire until just now."

"I will kill you," Scott said, and I flung out an arm to press him back as Reed caught him on the other side. "You son of a bitch, *I will kill you!*"

"You hang on to that happy thought as I'm pulling your guts out in long strings," Weissman said. He sounded deliriously pleased. "And then tying them to your girlfriend's thigh as a garter for her upcoming nuptials."

"He's after you," Zollers said suddenly from beside me. "You're priority one."

"Of course I'm after her," Weissman said, scoffing. "Do you realize how completely ineffectual the rest of you would be without her? She's the linchpin of your entire ridiculous operation. Without her, half of you would be hiding under your beds," he sent a glare at Scott, "and the other half would have charged blindly into whatever net we threw out to snare you. Of course, it's not looking like her leadership is going to do too much to keep you out of it …" He just grinned, like the cat that ate the canary.

I glanced at Zollers and he nodded. He knew what I was thinking, what I'd asked him:

If I run, will Weissman chase me?

His nod was all the affirmation I needed. I took a breath and turned to Reed. He was still standing there, holding Scott back with me. Our eyes met, and I could feel his hesitation. I wondered if we could communicate just by a look, if it would be enough. He shook his head, firmly. I could see his quiet refusal.

"Reed," I said, and tried to send every ounce of emotion, of pleading, of begging. All of their lives were in his hands, now, and their fates were tied to what he did next. "Please."

"You really should be begging me," Weissman said. You could tell he thought he'd already won, and it grated. "If you think—"

A howling of the wind blew hard all around me. I looked back and saw four of them; four enormous, swirling tornadoes launch my companions into the air. I watched them fly, two hundred feet straight up, and on a long, lazy arc away from where I stood staring down Weissman and his cronies.

"Son of a …" Weissman said, and his voice was tinged with annoyance. I could see the scowl on his face in the shadow cast by his headlights as I turned on my heel and sprinted away, back toward the conservatory entrance. “You have got to be kidding me. Go ahead and run, kid! Just savor the fear a little while longer, because your friends can’t escape from me … and it’ll be a fun night hunting you down first.”

Chapter 40

I had a head start, but not much of one. I could hear the two big guys following behind me. Something about them was entirely too familiar—not in a good way—and I wondered what it was.

I glanced back as I passed the conservatory entrance and kept going. The entry to the Como zoo was just a little farther, and my—admittedly limited—plan called for me to try and lose them inside.

The cool night air whipped across my face, and the faint smell of animals hung in my nose. My breaths were coming quick and sharp, more from the anticipation and fear than because I was winded.

I hung a hard right on the wide sidewalk that led into the zoo and pulled my gun, firing three times into the pane of glass to the side of the doors. The pane collapsed in big shards as I jumped through the empty space they'd left behind. I fired thrice more on the other side and shot through that pane as well seconds later.

I almost couldn't feel my feet, I was running so hard. I charged toward an exhibit building up ahead and looked back. The two guys were just behind me. I wondered briefly why Weissman didn't just freeze time and let them take hold of me before realizing the answer.

He wanted to hunt me. To spend the time stalking me, making me fear him. My friends were already as good as dead the minute he had his hands on me.

He was just savoring this.

I shot twice at the big guy following me closest. He had red hair that flooded off the top of his head, wavy and curly and flowing down his back, I could see that much in the torchlight. If the bullets hurt him, he gave no sign, just kept coming.

I swore and ran into the building ahead. It was shadowed, but I heard the faint sound of a monkey as I dodged inside.

I ducked into a dark area and realized I had, in fact, reached the monkey house. A chattering sound reached my ears from a nearby glass enclosure.

"Amazing isn't it?" Weissman's voice reached me from a few feet away. I turned and saw him in the shadows for a second, and then he was gone. "We evolved from them to become the dominant form of life on the planet." Now his voice was coming from somewhere else, bouncing off the walls, echoing through the monkey house. There was more chattering now as the denizens of the house responded to his voice. "Now we look down on them—and rightfully so—even though we once might have been the same."

"I don't see much difference between them and you," I said under my breath. "Though it's kind of dark in here; they're probably prettier than you."

"Hahah!" Weissman's laughter echoed. I suspected he'd found the most acoustically perfect place to taunt me from. He really was just playing games. "I find it a lot easier to bear your stupid insults when I know you're cornered. When you're caged. Like one of them." Somewhere he rapped on the glass, and it echoed. "Humans are like this to our kind, they just don't realize it. We're superior in every way, but for some reason we feel a need to hide among them. Like the fact that we're special, that we're better, should ever be hidden?"

"I don't see how you're that much better than them, especially in the area of hair care," I said, putting my back against a stone wall. The shadows were moving in here, but I couldn't hear much of anything over the chattering. It smelled, the strong scent of animal waste blocking out all else.

"Again with the goading," he said, and I thought I caught a

twinge of impatience again. I wasn't sure whether taunting him was going to be the key to making him draw this out or if it'd be the thing that would cause him to snap and put an end to it sooner, but I was having trouble stopping myself in either case. "But then again, you've always been blind to the truths right in front of your face. So busy coming up with the next smart thing to say that you miss all the obvious things you should notice."

"Tell me more," I said, looking around. I had a feeling the big guys were in here with me, but I couldn't see them.

"You looking for my tall friends?" Weissman said. "They're here. Closing in on you a little at a time."

"Cool," I said and pushed myself harder against the wall, trying to look left and right, keep my approaches covered. "Let me know when they're ready for a fight. My hands were bared, palms sweating, but if I could get my hands on them for about twenty uninterrupted seconds, I could put them away.

"Oh, they're ready to fight," he said. "They've got a little bit of a score to settle with you."

"Really?" I asked. "I don't remember beating the shit out of Sasquatch anytime in recent memory. Pray tell, what did I do to offend them? Did I insult their mother?"

"No," Weissman said with a chuckle. "You killed their brother."

I felt the chill creep down my spine as he said it, and the memory slammed home. The shadow moved to my left, and then to my right, and they swept in on me from both sides before I could do anything to react. As their faces crossed into the light for just the briefest of seconds, I knew why they had seemed so familiar before.

Those teeth. Those eyes. They were just like him.

Just like their brother.

Just like Wolfe.

Chapter 41

I dove hard, rolling into a shaft of light as I heard the Wolfe brothers behind me, stopping just before they plowed into each other. Fluorescent lights flickered overhead and flashed on, presumably thanks to Weissman monkeying with them somewhere.

I stared at the brothers Wolfe. The one on the left was the redhead, with a full, red beard and long, curly red hair coming down in strings around his face. He looked more human than Wolfe, but that wasn't a high bar to clear.

"Elmo!" I said to him. "You've really let yourself go to hell."

The other one was darker haired, but completely clean-shaven. He had short hair, but it was barely styled, just a mess that looked a little like he'd run his fingers through it to make it wild. I could see the hints of stubble across his cheeks. "And you, uh …"

"Save it," the dark-haired one said.

"We're not interested in your jibes, Nealon," the red-haired one said.

"Hey, you guys can actually speak without using the third person," I said, keeping on the balls of my toes. "Color me impressed."

They glanced at each other, bereft of any amusement.

"I should probably introduce you," Weissman said. "This is Grihm." The red-haired one smiled, his pointed teeth revealed. "And Frederick." The clean-shaven one nodded his head slightly.

I stared. "Frederick? Seriously?"

"I like it," Frederick said, and I was surprised at how there was no growl in his voice. He sounded … almost normal. Almost. "It sounds cultured."

"Also, it's multi-syllabic, which is definitely bucking the family trend," I said. I was surveying them and running my mouth off in hopes that we could delay the fighting just a little longer. If these two were anything like Wolfe, this was not going to be pretty. Wolfe was well nigh invulnerable to bullets, and I was pretty sure Grihm had proven earlier that it ran in the family.

That left me draining them to death, like I had their brother. But I had my doubts Weissman would let that happen without intervening.

I glanced around. Where was Weissman? I had heard him a moment earlier, and I knew he had to be just waiting to swoop in if things somehow went wrong with Grihm and Frederick. Plus there was Claire, still somewhere out there.

"So," I said, trying to kill a little more time, "I take it you boys heard what I did to your brother?"

There was an utter lack of reaction from either of them at first, and then Frederick nodded slightly, a grim smile spreading over his face. "Drank him dry, didn't you?"

"Something like that." If they knew how I'd killed him, they were almost certain not to make it easy on me. I wondered how exactly I was supposed to kill them if they already knew to guard against the only sure method I had.

"Here's something you don't know," Grihm said, sweeping his red hair out of his eyes with his hand. His fingernails were long and clawed, like Wolfe's, but they were impeccably kept, like he went for regular manicures at the groomers. "We killed your aunt. And James Fries."

"Uhm …" I thought about what to say to that. "Thank you, I think?"

They exchanged a look. Frederick spoke. "We assumed you'd be unhappy about that."

I had a lot of emotions running through me; if I was unhappy about them killing Charlie and James, it was in way distant last place, somewhere past fear for my friends, for myself and for my entire surviving race. I was far more worried about how the next five or ten minutes were going to play out, frankly. "Well, you know what they say about assuming."

Frederick frowned at me. Actually frowned. No growl at all. "You're a very sarcastic person. I suspect it's stunting your emotional growth."

"What. The. Hell?" Did I just get psychoanalyzed by a Wolfe brother? I could feel some displeasure somewhere deep inside, from Wolfe himself. A choice comment about Frederick being a smug asshole floated my way from within.

Grihm crossed in front of Frederick, and both of them realigned to put me at the center of a ninety-degree angle. I knew they were going to leap, I just didn't know when. They both tensed, but I was staring at them, one eye on each, trying to decide how this was going to play out. I suspected not good. The odds were not so much in my favor, after all.

They leapt and I pre-empted them, charging at Frederick. I went low, aiming to chop block his leg with my shoulder. It felt like an iron rod slammed into my collarbone as he landed a knee on me. I tried to muscle through but it didn't work so well. He countered by bringing down a fist like a hammer on the top of my head, and I was forced to dodge right to avoid taking any more damage from him.

"Maybe you thought just because we seem smarter and more well-spoken than our brother, we're worse fighters than him?" This from Frederick, whose blow to my head still had me seeing stars.

"I lived in hope, yes," I said, keeping my distance. They were back to standing off, in balanced stances that told me they were ready to leap.

"Now you can learn to live in fear," Weissman said from somewhere far behind me. I thought about looking back, but it was pointless to focus on him. He was going to let this play out. Let me get humiliated. "It'll be good practice for you for what's to come."

"Ah, yes, my arranged marriage," I said, glaring back at Grihm and Frederick. "I can't tell you how excited I am about that."

"Your emotional state is more or less irrelevant," Weissman said, and I could tell he meant it.

"Clearly the key to every successful marriage," I said. "Right up there with despising your intended's friends." I looked from Grihm to Frederick. "We're really covering all the bases here."

"You'll get over it," Frederick said, his dark head bobbing as he maintained his fighting stance.

"Given time, you'll probably come to realize how perfect for each other you and Sovereign are," Grihm added. He was smiling under that red beard.

"And if I don't?" I didn't really care what they thought, but I was delaying again. This fight was going to suck unless I could lay hands on a missile launcher. Hell, even if I could.

"That sounds like your problem, not ours," Frederick said.

"We're just here to help arrange the wedding," Grihm said. "The honeymoon and everything that follows is between you and a counselor of your choosing. Though I'd suggest you avoid Dr. Phil."

"Stall all you want," Weissman said, his voice echoing down the hall. "Your campus is my next stop after I have you packaged and ready to ship, so don't think you're doing anything other than delaying your friends' painful and impending deaths." I could hear him chuckle from wherever he was perched. "I'm gonna have a lot of fun with that boyfriend of yours before he dies. Do you have any idea how much I hated his aunt and uncle? Enough that I made their murder scene unintentionally look like Wolfe's handiwork, that's how much. I figure I can do at least that much courtesy to him when the moment comes—"

I felt a surge of rage and leapt at Grihm, who was nearest to me. His eyes didn't even widen as I came at him. I hit him in the jaw with my lead-off punch then landed another in his belly.

He did not even flinch. Just stood there and grinned through his feral teeth. "My turn."

I had no time to dodge his offhand jab, and I honestly don't know if I could have even if I'd had ample warning. Grihm was fast, faster than anyone else I could recall fighting, and his hand hit me in the nose like I'd had a piano fall on my head. I heard my nose break, felt it crack. Warm blood spilled down my lips as I staggered back.

"Don't kill her," Weissman said mildly, his voice seeming to come from all around me. "Or remove anything that won't grow back. Everything else is fair game."

"Sovereign … won't be too happy … if you hurt me," I said through the blood running down my lips. There were stars flashing in my eyes.

"I think he knows that you can't make an omelet without breaking a few eggs," Weissman said. "Besides, we'll hose you off before we hand you over, make sure you have time for the bruises and bite marks to heal."

I blinked as another monstrous punch came my way, this time from Frederick. I saw it in my peripheral vision just before it landed and barely inclined my head in order to mitigate the damage. It still sent me staggering; this time right into Grihm's waiting paws. He slashed me hard across the belly and I felt my skin open with a screaming pain, felt blood run down my shirt and belly.

"Hmm," Frederick said. "That's just what I did to Charlie. It's kind of poetic, or perhaps even a little symmetrical, in a way."

I couldn't have opened my mouth without screaming or I might have asked if it was symmetrical because I was folded in half, clutching at my belly. One of them elbowed me in the back of the head before I could get upright again, and I hit the floor, hard.

The smell of blood and monkey dung hung in my nose. The tangy flavor of the blood was heavy in my mouth. I could see one of the Wolfe brothers' trunk-like legs standing in front of me and I reached out for it, grasping at the cuff of his pants. If I could just pull it aside to get to the skin—

"Nuh uh," Frederick said. Or was it Grihm? Someone punched me in the kidney hard enough that I was sure they'd broken my back or burst my internal organs or maybe just caused my entire upper body to explode.

My face pressed against the concrete floor as I lay there. I could hear the maddening thunder of my blood pumping in my ears. I tried to roll, but something was stopping me. A heavy weight was on my back, keeping me down.

A giggle sounded just in front of me, and I raised my eyelids just enough to see Weissman standing there, stooped over, to look me in the eye. "I gotta admit, this was a little disappointing. It wasn't like a fight. It was like I threw a bunny into a cage with two rabid dogs—" He looked up. "No offense, boys."

"None taken," Grihm said.

"A little taken," Frederick replied.

"—and you just … you couldn't even go one round," Weissman said. His grin was so wide, it eclipsed all the other details of his face. "But then again, you always were out of your depth. You know why? Because all this time, we've been planning, and strategizing, and preparing … and all you've done is run, and react, and use up every last ounce of luck you've ever had." He punched me hard, in the kidney, where one of the Wolfe brothers had landed a world-ending blow just a few moments before, and it hurt so much I was sure I would bleed to death internally. "Guess what, princess? Your luck's finally run out."

He stood, and all I could see were his black shoes. “Now bind her up and let’s take her to the airport … I’ve got still got a long, painful night of business to attend to with her friends.”

Chapter 42

I was unconscious for most of the ride, only dimly aware of my surroundings. My hands had been bound with barbed wire, and it burned every time I moved them. A slow series of moans worked its way free from my lips against my will, entirely involuntarily. My face was mashed against the rough fabric of the trunk of Weissman's car, and in between forced, gasping breaths of blood, I wondered if I would ever see my mother alive again. Or Scott. Or Reed. Or …

A vague thumping sound came to me as I drifted in and out of wakefulness. I couldn't tell if it was the car hitting speed bumps or something else. I wondered if we were shifting in and out of time as we drove. Badly beaten as I was, I couldn't tell. Being awake for more than a few seconds felt like a struggle.

We came to a stop and a final loud thump jarred me mostly awake. Everything ached, especially my back, and I wondered if I had a broken spine. I could still feel my toes, so I supposed not.

There were muted voices outside, and then I heard a click as the trunk sprang open. I wanted to jump through it, force myself to my feet and start running. My body failed to obey, though, the pains and agonies gripping me still screaming through every nerve ending in my body.

"Help me …" I whispered, not sure who I was calling out to. "Please …"

"No one to help you now," Grihm said, his smug face appearing above me. His clawed hands reached into the trunk and I felt the tips of his fingers grasp hold of me and draw blood as he dragged me out.

"Your brother died screaming like a little bitch," I said as he stood me up, hooking his arm under mine. I looked up and saw a hangar around us and a plane in the center of it, an old propeller-based one that looked like it hauled cargo. The smell of oil was thick in the air, overcoming the blood still dripping in my nostrils.

"That sounds like him, all right," Grihm said with a shrug. I caught sight of Frederick a couple paces off, and he nodded.

"You don't even care?" I asked. Grihm had me; he was entirely supporting my weight, like my legs were refusing to work at all.

"Nope," Frederick answered for him. "There's a reason we weren't with him when he died." He laughed. "Let's face it; Wolfe was a lowbrow, unsophisticated asshole. The family dunce, really."

"And you guys are so much different from him," I snapped.

"We are," Grihm said.

"We beat you, after all," Frederick said with a grin of his own. The lack of hair on his face made him look even less human as he said it. "Wolfe died trying, the big sub-human pussy."

I felt a stir of anger within that wasn't from me. "If you hated him that much, why are you so all-fired eager to hurt me?"

"There's a difference between hating your brother and wanting him dead," Frederick said, and he punched me in the gut as Grihm paraded me past. I heard something pop inside, and I was sure it was something important.

"Yeah," Grihm said as I got a really good view of the hangar floor. My belly cried out from the damage Frederick had done to me, and it—or something else—was keeping me from standing upright. I felt the harsh ripping of skin on my wrists as he tore the razor wire free. "Here we are—your new home. I bet it looks familiar."

I raised my head to look at where he'd carried me. As soon as I did, I wished I hadn't.

There was a dark metal box standing open in front of me,

slightly narrower and shallower than the one that my mother had imprisoned me in as a child. The glistening of the metal told me it was something more solid than steel, that the thickness of the walls was plenty enough to keep me from breaking down the door as I had in my old prison. It shone in the half-lit darkness of the hangar, and the thrumming note of panic and pain in my gut became a screaming chorus.

I tried to make my legs work, but they wouldn't. I tried to writhe out of Grihm's hold on me but to no avail. I could only turn my head, and when I pushed it to one side I saw the hangar doors open wide, the dark night and the runway lit up outside. When I turned the other way, I realized why I couldn't move my body.

"Hi there," Claire said, waving to me with the tips of her fingers. "Having a little trouble with your basic motor skills?" I wanted to punch her so hard she'd need assistance doing everything including toileting for the rest of her life. "Tsk-tsk," she said. "It took a good day for me to walk normally after what you did to my leg. This is only going to last for as long as it takes these boys to get you in your new home." She waved again and turned off. "Ta ta!"

I heard a hard slapping hit and glanced back to see Claire hit the ground. Something snapped and she fell like she was dead.

"What the hell?" Frederick said. "How'd you get here?"

"I rode the bumper," my mother said, standing over Claire's fallen form.

"How'd you keep the telepath from detecting you?" Grihm asked.

"I presume I had a little long-distance help from a stronger telepath," my mother said with a wary smile. "Now then … which of you dies first?"

There was a flash behind my mother and something appeared in her chest, right in the middle, beneath her sternum.

A blade. Sticking out of the center of her chest.

"Off the top of my head, mommy dearest," Weissman said from just behind her shoulder, his grin stretching from ear to ear, "I'm going to say … you."

Chapter 43

SIERRA

Sierra Nealon felt her legs give way, the metallic tang of blood bubbling on her lips. Her hands shook, and her legs fell from underneath her. She could feel the blade poking through her chest, knew it had penetrated the heart. Cleaved it.

"Oh, mommy," Weissman whispered in her ear. "Poor mommy. It was really stupid to come here instead of staying with the others. You never stood chance, after all. Time … was never on your side." He was entirely too gleeful about it.

Sierra tried to burble something out, but her breath didn't come, and she struggled.

"Oh, you're still alive!" Weissman said. "Barely, it's true, but I can work with that." He slid the blade out of her back—slowly, agonizingly slowly, and she felt every inch of it as he did it. "I can make it last a while. But first …" He turned his head, and Sierra felt herself crumple face-first to the hard concrete floor. She barely felt it. "Get her loaded."

It took Sierra a moment to realize that the "her" being mentioned was not her, but Sienna. She tried to turn her head to look. Sienna. The breaths were coming raspy now. Had the blade hit her lungs, too? How was that possible? Or was it just—

Her logical mind tried to apply her medical training to what she felt, but her brain wouldn't cooperate. She could see Sienna now, silent, horrified, with that look on her face like she'd gotten when she was a kid in over her head on something. She'd gotten it that time she'd fallen down the slide in Des Moines, and it had sounded like she'd hit hard enough to break something. That had been scary. That had been the look on her face, too, when she was four years old. It hadn't changed.

Sienna's face hadn't ever really changed. She was still just a girl. Sierra gasped and tried to roll. Could she crawl? She could damned well try. Her face was pressed against the concrete floor. She'd die trying. She'd known it was coming anyway.

"So …" Weissman said, and Sierra could see the back of his head. The Wolfe brothers had Sienna in the box now. Sierra wanted to laugh and cry at the same time over the irony, but she had put all her effort into crawling toward her daughter. Every inch she moved hurt like she was ripping her own heart out. For all she knew, she was. "Feel homey?"

Sienna was stood up, leaned against the back wall of the box. Probably didn't have control of her limbs yet. Not that it would matter. Sierra could see the Wolfe brothers hovering, waiting for her to try something. Sierra doubted she could. That telepath was strong; whatever she'd done might not have worn off even after Sierra knocked her the hell out.

Sienna didn't answer. That was the right option from Sierra's point of view. Bide her time. Don't waste energy sniping with shots that wouldn't do any good. She thought about it for a second; Sienna's power of speech was probably gone. There was no way she'd shut up and take this indignity in silence.

"Now," Weissman said, in a voice dripping with glee, "you're going to take a little plane ride. This crate will keep you out of trouble during your flight, and maybe—just maybe—if you're good … the boys will let you out for a walk when you get where you're going." He cackled. "Maybe not. I mean, you're going to Sovereign, but no one says you have to go to him right away, if you know what I mean." He laughed again. "You know what I mean. Because you deserve a few weeks of beatings and whatnot before you get to him. It'll probably improve your disposition, learning who's the boss."

It had never worked before, Sierra thought, still inching forward. There was an awful lot of blood pumping out of her. An awful lot. It was pooling out at an alarming rate.

"Get her out of here," Weissman said, and Sierra looked up just in time to see them shut the door to the box. It was a familiar view, one she'd seen from the outside more times than she could count. Every single one of them was followed by a gut-wrenching, sickening feeling of regret.

But this one was the worst of all.

She pulled harder, and a little wash of blood burbled out of her lips. The plane's back ramp was down, and Weissman was just standing there as the Wolfe brothers dragged the box up the ramp. It rattled along the uneven deck of the plane, ringing out with each thump as they dragged her daughter away from her.

"No," she whispered, and a mouthful of blood poured out on the concrete.

"Oh, it's you," Weissman said. He was staring down at her from a few feet away, as though she were some object unworthy of his interest. Like she were lower than low. Lower than him. She wanted to rip his legs from beneath him, bury her teeth in his jugular— "You just don't know when to give up, do you?"

Weissman shook his head, then looked back over his shoulder. Now was her chance. "Close the ramp and take off, will you? And take your time with her. Beatings every day, maybe a vivisection a couple times a week. Make her suffer. I'll let you know when you can turn her over to Sovereign." A sideways smile broke across his profile, and Sierra wanted to break all of his teeth out. All of them. "It might be a while."

She was almost to him. Almost there. The ramp of the airplane was rising, but she couldn't focus on that now. She had to kill Weissman. It was why she was here, her sole reason for existing on this day, at this moment. She reached out, and took hold of his pants leg-—

He looked down at her. "God, still you, huh? You've got guts, I'll give you that." He grinned. "Now let's cut them out before you die." He tugged at his leg, but she did not relinquish it, holding tight to the hem of his pants. "Oh, now you're just annoying me. Fine, I'll—"

His eyes grew wide, and his jaw fell open. "How—what the—how are you doing that?" He bent over, staring at her hand. "You're not even touching me, there's no way you could be stopping me from halting time and—" He stopped, flustered, face red. "Fine. We'll do this the old fashioned way." His hand reached behind his back—

Sierra pulled with all her fury, all her strength, and ripped his leg from the ground. Weissman tottered, one leg left to stand on, and Sierra struck out with her hand. She could hear his ankle snap from the perfect placement of her strike, years of training funneled into this moment.

He landed hard upon his back and let out a cry. She could hear the grinding of the plane's gears as the propellers spun up in the front. She didn't waste time looking to see if the ramp was closed; she had no time to spare. Sierra pulled herself along Weissman's fallen body as he struggled. She punched him hard enough in the groin for his ancestors to feel it then did it again for good measure. The sound of popping tissue and his screams were all the encouragement she needed to keep going.

She crawled along the length of him while he struggled and stopped at his throat. He was struggling against her weight, against the way she had him pinned. She saw his hand break free from behind his back, brandishing the knife he'd been carrying in his back waistband.

If she were some new trainee, facing down a man in a knife while she was bleeding out, she might have panicked. Especially given the stakes. But she was Sierra Nealon, by God, and she'd known this was going to happen. She'd trained her whole adult life to fight like this, to do the things no one else was willing to do in order to be the best. Discipline was everything. She was iron.

And Weissman was a cream puff.

She caught his hand before he even got it around. He was so slow. His face was thick with fear, like he couldn't believe this was happening to him. She cracked his wrist—something so basic a novice student of Aikido would have known how to escape it—and he dropped the knife. She snatched it up.

"Looks like … you're out of time …" she whispered, voice guttural, as she ran it across his throat.

If she'd been in his place, she could have stopped it. But he was weak, this Weissman. Fat. Undisciplined. She could see the rage that drove him as she opened his neck. Rage was good, but it couldn't win every battle for you.

Cold discipline beat hot rage every time.

She watched the light fade from his eyes even as hers grew heavy. She rolled off of him after nearly sawing his head off and stopped when she saw the feet standing in front of her. Did they come from the plane?

No.

She stared up at the man above her, and she knew him. She'd seen him before. "Shin'ichi Akiyama," she breathed. She knew she didn't have many breaths remaining.

"Sierra Nealon, I presume?" Akiyama stooped, squatting low to speak to her. "I am surprised that you know me."

"We've met before," Sierra said. "Last time we spoke, some fourteen years ago, you told me, 'The next time we meet will be on the day you die. But your death will save your daughter's life.'"

"It would appear I have further to travel back," Akiyama said, slow and pensive. Why was he so pensive? She'd just told him everything he needed to know, hadn't she? "And here I had thought my debt was paid in full."

"No," she said, shaking her head. All the luster had gone out of the world and darkness was seeping in from outside the hangar. The plane was gone, and she wondered for how long. "Sienna …?"

"I have an appointment with her in a few years," Akiyama said with a light smile. "On that occasion, she will remember me, but I will have no memory of her." He inclined his head slightly. "It sounds as though you and I have a similar appointment."

"Can you …" The thoughts were coming slower now, and so were the breaths. "… Can you … is there anything … you can do for me …?"

"I am afraid I cannot," Akiyama said. "I am limited in my power to affect the events of this—my past. I could only do what I have done because it was already destined to happen. As is our next meeting, it would appear, the one in which you will meet me for the very first time."

"I … can't … don't want to leave … Sienna …" Sierra's emotions broke loose, and the fear, oh God, the fear, it drowned everything else out.

"Be at peace, Sierra Nealon," Akiyama said, and his hand brushed her cheek. She could feel wetness there. "Your fight is over now."

She could feel the slow hiss of that last breath, and the dimness sunk in. She couldn't speak to say her last, couldn't get the words out. She could still hear him, though, the last thing he said before she felt the world fade away.

"But your daughter's fight … I am afraid it is just beginning …"

Chapter 44

SIENNA

I had watched Weissman close the door to the front of the box numbly, my mother dead on the ground somewhere behind him. I had watched him take her life with a mixture of paralysis and rage, and words had failed me.

Now I felt only the darkness close in on me as the box thumped up the ramp of the plane, each hit it took like another nail being driven into my coffin.

My mother was dead.

My freedom was lost.

Weissman was going to kill everyone I cared about.

Then he was going to wipe out the remainder of my species and enslave all mankind.

If I was honest with myself—really honest—the first three of those felt far more immediate and horrible than the last one, if only because I could personally taste the consequences of my failure. And they were the bitterest tonic I could remember since the day I'd held Zack in my arms after he died. That last consequence was a creature of the future.

And right now I didn't have a future.

I sobbed openly as I felt the box locked into place, held upright by chains or a cargo net to keep me from toppling over.

"Awww," came the mocking voice of Grihm just outside. "Listen to her cry. Can you believe she killed Wolfe?"

"Yeah," Frederick said. "He always was a weakling, physically and intellectually. The runt of our litter—metaphorically speaking."

Somewhere outside, I could hear their low guffaws over the engines of the aircraft throttling up. Everything broke loose inside me, a torrent of emotions—rage, frustration, sadness—that allowed a voice to escape the back of my mind.

Little Doll ... the Wolfe has changed his mind. The Wolfe will help you kill them all. Just for fun. Them and Sovereign and Weissman and—

"Do you know how to make my body use your powers?" I asked, choking back a sob.

There was a long pause. *Not ... really,* Wolfe finally said. *But—*

I could feel my eyes, sticky, puckering shut. "Then what the hell is the point?" I didn't even bother to slam the door on him; he just wandered out of my view. All of them wandered around back there, free from their cages, not saying anything. They were probably happy.

Not all of us, Zack said.

I sobbed again, helpless against the fear. My life was over. My destiny was to be tortured for fun until Sovereign "rescued" me, whenever that would be. I was caged like I had been as a child. Stuck in place, in a box, just like …

A memory tumbled loose. Something stirred by my thoughts of myself—a girl, trapped in stasis.

… just like Andromeda.

Andromeda …? I hadn't really thought of her in forever, but something she said floated to the top of my mind unbidden and gave me a chill.

I had watched the blood spread over her chest, and she spoke: *"Remember me when you are cast back into the darkness, and I will light your way—I will show you the way."*

I took a desperate, hopeful breath of the metallic air. The blood on my face and in my mouth had dried, leaving a crust behind. I scratched at it with my fingers, took another breath, and listened. All I could hear outside was the plane's engines. If we hadn't taken off yet, we were about to.

"Andromeda?" I whispered the name uncertainly, afraid I'd be heard. "Please. Help me. Andromeda …"

I waited, and heard …

Nothing.

I slumped against the hard metal wall and felt a tear drip down my cheek. My face crumpled, and I hated myself as I sat there in the dark, isolated, cut off. Fated to this darkness, to the cage, like the prisoner I was. Brought to this purpose so I could be nothing more than a sacrifice to a powerful man, to be disposed of at his whim, just like—

I raised my head and another thought occurred to me. The chill came back.

Just like Andromeda?

No …

Not Andromeda. Just like …

"Adelaide." I said her name aloud. Remembered seeing her die at the hands of Wolfe … and then heard a voice deep within.

No, Little Doll, Wolfe said. *Not die. Close ... but not dead.*

"Adelaide," I said, whispering the name again.

I felt another stir inside. Something barely moving deep within.

A shadow. The barest fragment of a soul passed to me by a touch over a year ago.

"Andromeda … wasn't your real name," I said, the cold breath of hope stirring me. "Adelaide. Your name was Adelaide before … before whatever Omega did to you."

I could feel it, the barest breath, and then the answer came back to me in the form of a voice I hadn't heard in over a year. A shadow, sliding out of the darkness of my past … exactly like she had promised me she would before she died.

Hello, Sienna Nealon ... I have been waiting for this moment ...

... I have been waiting here in the darkness ...

... for you.

Thanks for reading *Destiny: The Girl in the Box, Book 9*. I hope you enjoyed it!

Would you like to know when my next book is available? You can sign up for my new release e-mail alerts, you can follow me on Twitter - *@robertJcrane*, or Like my Facebook page at *robertJcrane (Author)* or you can email me at cyrusdavidon@gmail.com.

This was the ninth book in the Girl in the Box Series. Here's a list of all the books in the series, in order:

Alone: The Girl in the Box, Book One
Untouched: The Girl in the Box, Book Two
Soulless: The Girl in the Box, Book Three
Family: The Girl in the Box, Book Four
Omega: The Girl in the Box, Book Five
Broken: The Girl in the Box, Book Six
Enemies: The Girl in the Box, Book Seven
Legacy: The Girl in the Box, Book Eight
Power: The Girl in the Box, Book Ten* (Coming Summer 2014!)

Limitless: Out of the Box, Book One* (Coming Late 2014/Early 2015!)

Yes, there is going to be a sequel series. The main storyline with Sovereign is going to wrap up in book 10, but the series has a very big world, and there are a lot of things I want to delve deeper into. For example, there's obviously a story with Akiyama, and it's not something I can fit into the Girl in the Box series by the end. But I will deal with it in Out of the Box (#6, in case you're curious).

Reviews help other readers find books. If you enjoyed the book and could take a moment to post a short review on the website you brought it from, tell a friend, tweet about it or mention it on your Facebook page, I'd greatly appreciate it. If you did all four I'd be super-duper-extra grateful.

Other Works by Robert J. Crane

The Sanctuary Series

Epic Fantasy

Defender: The Sanctuary Series, Volume One

Avenger: The Sanctuary Series, Volume Two

Champion: The Sanctuary Series, Volume Three

Crusader: The Sanctuary Series, Volume Four

Sanctuary Tales, Volume One - A Short Story Collection

Thy Father's Shadow: (Sanctuary 4.5)* (Coming Summer 2014!)

Master: The Sanctuary Series, Volume Five* (Coming 2014)

Southern Watch

Contemporary Urban Fantasy

Called: Southern Watch, Book 1

Depths: Southern Watch, Book 2

Corrupted: Southern Watch, Book 3* (Coming Summer 2014!)

* *Forthcoming*

Made in the USA
Coppell, TX
23 March 2020